Triangles

3

NIA RICH

Also by Nia Rich

Never Going Back

My Love Is Deeper

F--k Boy

Lovers Remorse

Seduced by a Savage

Triangles 3

Written by: Nia Rich
Copyright © 2017 Nia Rich

All rights reserved.

Cover: Tina Louise
Editor: Venitia Crawford

Triangles

3

Previously in Triangles….

Raelyn

I heard my phone ringing again and I knew that it was my sister, but Laron was in the middle of putting chocolate syrup all over my toes to suck it off. Riley had called me the night before, but I was with Laron, so I didn't answer. I watched Laron sucking my toes like they were the best ice cream sundae he's ever eaten. I promised myself that I would call my sister back after I got the best sex ever from Laron.

I smiled at Laron as he was gently massaging my toes with his mouth and tongue.

"You like that don't you baby?" Laron asked.

"Yes, I do." I replied. He finished sucking the chocolate off my toes and begin kissing up my legs towards me.

"I bought you a new toy." he said.

I smiled and said, "Really?"

"Yep. It has three different speeds and ten different pulse settings. I figured it should keep you busy when I am not around."

"Awww thank you baby." I said.

"You're welcome. I'll give it to you before I leave tomorrow." he said and then he kissed my thigh.

I said, "New York should be amazing."

"Yup as soon as you get there. You got the ticket I bought you?"

"Yes. They are in a safe place."

"Good. I'm glad that you decided to come and spend a couple of days with me. Don't forget, I got a shoot to do in Cali when we leave N.Y. so I will meet you back here in Minnesota when that is done."

"When do I get to see your new place?"

"As soon as I finish furnishing it. I got a court date when I get back to finalize this divorce and then I am all yours."

I smiled before saying, "I should tell you now. I think that I may be pregnant." I knew that I had just casually hit him with a bombshell, but there was no better time like the present.

Laron paused and looked at me. "What?" he asked.

I said, "Yes. My period is late."

"Oh, wow baby."

He gave me a nervous smile and scratched his head.

"I know. I felt the same way. I mean, I know that you are going through a divorce, so if you don't want to keep it I understand."

"No baby, I would never tell you to do that."

"When do you find out?"

"I planned to take a test before flying out to New York."

"Alright, well let me know. Either way, you're my baby and we are going to be each other's soon. I got you."

"Ok." I said.

I smiled and watched him bury his head between my legs. I tilted my head back and let him take me to another place with his mouth and tongue.

***

My bed felt so much better with Laron in it. I loved having him around and thoughts about a future with him had been swirling around in my mind. I wasn't thinking about a baby, but being with Laron everyday was something that I was growing excited about.

After we made love, we passed out in each other's arms in my bed. I toss and turn in my sleep, so sometimes during the night, I would end up outside of his arms with my back turned towards him. I stirred in my sleep a little and then I turned to wrap my arms around Laron. I felt something near me, so I opened my eyes. Paris was standing right by my bed, in the dark, dressed in all black, with a gun pointed at Laron. She was standing silently with the evilest scowl on her face.

I jumped and yelled, "Oh my God!"

Paris didn't flinch, but my yell made Laron Jerk awake.

"Wha- Oh shit! Paris?" he yelled.

"Surprise mutha fucka." Paris said.

"What are you doing here? How did you get in here?" Laron asked.

"Never underestimate a bitch that can pick a lock. You might want to put a chain on the door when you're out creeping on your wife. What are you doing here? I thought you were supposed to be in New York. That's what you told me, right?"

She slowly moved closer to him pressing the gun into his chest. I watched quietly with fear in my eyes and my cover pulled over my naked body. I don't know why I was covering up. It wasn't like she had never seen me naked. I guess it made me feel protected from her gun.

"Cool out Paris." he said.

"I'm supposed to be cool when my husband is in another woman's bed. The woman that you told me that we were done with?"

"What?" I asked. My face immediately frowned.

"Yes." Paris said to me without looking at me. She had her eyes on Laron and the gun in his chest.

"Paris baby, you are tripping right now."

"You have been lying to me, and you really thought that I wouldn't find out?"

She stepped back and pointed the gun at me. "And you. Really? You couldn't find your own man. You had to try and steal mine? I knew you were a shady bitch."

I said, Look, I don't have to steal nothing. Laron tell her."

"Baby, stop." he said to Paris.

"Tell her Laron. I didn't steal anything. You came to me."

"I-" Laron was tongue tied.

"You told me that you were getting a divorce." I said.

She pointed the gun back at Laron. "A divorce?! You've been coming home every night to me, telling me that you love me, but we're getting a divorce? Since when? And why didn't I know about this divorce Laron?!"

He was silent.

Paris continued, "You're a fucking liar. I've read everything. All your text messages. I put a GPS tracker on your phone. That is how I found you here, and you thought that you could get away with this."

She cocked the gun and aimed it at me.

I said, "Paris, I swear, I didn't know. I swear."

She pointed the gun back at Laron.

"You had the nerve to go behind my back after promising me that you would never do that."

Tears began streaming down her face. She kept the gun pointed at Laron while she took a cigarette from behind her ear and lit it with a lighter that she had in her pocket. I didn't know that Paris smoked up until that moment. She took a few heavy pulls from the cigarette and blew the smoke in the air as a river as tears continued to flow down her face.

Laron spoke slowly and quietly, "Baby listen, I'm sorry. Ok. Let's just go home and talk about it."

He was nervous, and I was nervous. I didn't know what she was going to do. It looked to me like she planned to kill both of us. I was praying that she was just there to scare him, and we would make it out of my bedroom alive. Paris stood silently smoking the cigarette like it was the last one she was ever going to have. She looked at me and then she looked at Laron, and then she said, "Fuck going home."

POW!

Triangles

3

NIA RICH

Triangles 3

"He's not with her. She is just jealous that he has moved on." - Riley

Chapter 1

Raelyn

"Ah shit Paris! You shot me!" Laron yelled as he grabbed his arm.

I jumped, but I stayed quiet. I didn't want to bring attention to myself and end up with a bullet in my ass. I was shaking and too scared to cry. I was in shock by what was happening. I didn't know what she was going to do next. She was bold enough to break into my home, and gangster enough to shoot her husband in my bed right in front of me. There is no telling if either one of us would make it through the situation alive. Paris took aim again, but this time she pointed at his crotch.

"I should shoot your mutha fuckin dick off for being the liar that you are." she said.

My eyes grew big. I was praying to myself that someone heard the first shot and called the police. I stayed quiet, but Laron began begging. "Please Paris baby, please don't. You already shot me. I am sure the cops are on the way. Please baby." he said while holding his arm.

"I don't, fucking, care, Laron." she said.

The look in her eyes said that she didn't give a fuck. I was preparing for the second shot to him, and then a third one to put an end to me. She glared at him for a moment, and then she took another hit from her cigarette causing the ash from it to fall to my floor. She put the gun down to her side, turned, and walked out of my room. I didn't move until I heard her walk out of my front door.

I jumped up and said, "Oh my God. Laron are you ok?"

"I don't know. You got to take me to the hospital."

He sat up still holding his arm. I ran to the door to lock and chain it. I began putting clothes on, and then I helped him get dressed. We left out of my apartment in a hurry. I was nervous walking down the hallway of my apartment building. It was eerily quiet, and I was sure that my neighbors hadn't heard a thing, or if they did, they had chosen to mind their own business. I didn't know if Paris was going to pop out of a corner ready to finish the job. We made it to my car with no sign of Paris anywhere. I was shaking the whole drive to Hennepin County Medical Center. It was two o'clock in the morning and I was ready to wake up from the nightmare.

Chapter 2

Paris

I didn't know where to go, so I went home to start packing some stuff, and then I gave up on packing. I sat down and started chain smoking cigarettes in the dark. I was drunk, pissed, emotional, and I didn't have the energy to try to run. I felt humiliated. I started thinking about all the good times Laron and I had; just to find out that he was cheating on me with the chick that I agreed to have in our bed. It was going on for almost six months. I felt like I should have listened to Priscilla when she told me not to do it, but I had to please my husband and spice up our marriage. I was in the middle of my fifth cigarette when I heard a loud knock at the door.

"Police! Open up!"

I stood up and walked to the door. I opened it. They slowly moved towards me and asked me if I had a weapon.

"Ma'am where is your weapon?"

"On the coffee table."

"We need you to come with us."

"Ok."

They didn't put me in handcuffs. They walked with me to the car and helped me into the back seat.

Chapter 3

Riley

Riley called Raelyn again. She was getting angry because it was unlike her sister to not answer the phone, and not return a call. She'd told herself that if her sister didn't answer again, she was going to stop over at her house to see what was going on. They both had to work that weekend and she wanted Raelyn to see her face before they got to work. She was surprised when her twin answered.

"Yo."

"Yo! Where the hell have you been!? I have been calling you!"

"I'm at the hospital."

"What!? What happened?"

"I'm fine. Laron's hurt. It's a long story. I'm exhausted. I've been up all night."

"I'm coming to you. What hospital are you at?"

"Hennepin County."

"I'll be there. Text me the details."

Riley hung up, grabbed her keys, and walked out of the door.

***

Riley made it to the hospital minutes later. She couldn't wait to see her sister, so she could tell her what happened and find out what was going on. Raelyn met Riley outside of Laron's hospital room.

"What happened?" Riley asked after they hugged.

Raelyn frowned and grabbed her sisters chin. "First off, what happened to you?" she asked as she looked at Riley's black eye.

Riley touched her eye and said, "This is why I've been calling you like crazy."

"Who did this to you?"

Riley sighed. "Jamir's wife."

"What?"

"Yes."

"When?"

"We should sit down."

Raelyn and Riley walked down the hall to the waiting room and sat down.

"Jamir's wife showed up at my door the other night and attacked me. He pulled her off me and I told them both to get away from my house."

"I thought he told you that he was no longer married?"

"He lied. His wife was pounding at my door screaming for her husband to come outside."

Raelyn bit her lip to stop from saying I told you so because her situation was no better.

"Well I guess it was the attack of the liars and crazy wives this week because the same thing happened to me."

"Laron's wife attacked you?"

"Well, she didn't do anything to me, but she broke into my house and shot him."

"No sister."

"Yes, while he was lying in my bed. It scared the hell out of me. I'm still shaken."

"Oh my God sister. I thought you were done with him."

"I was, but then he came to me and begged me to give him another chance, and told me that he was leaving her and I fell for it. Apparently, he was lying to both of us about each other. She found out and snapped. I could have lost my life, and Laron is lying up in a hospital bed."

"That bitch should be locked up in jail."

"Jamir's wife should be too. Look at your eye."

"At least I didn't almost die."

"You don't know what kind of shit his wife was on either."

"That is true. I'm glad that we're both alive sister."

"Me too. I'm gonna stick around here until they release him and then I'm done with his lying, cheating ass."

"I am too through with Jamir."

***

Riley heard her doorbell ringing. She dried her hands on the dish towel hanging from the cabinet below her and looked out of the kitchen window. She could see Jamir's car parked outside. She paused for moment and then she heard the doorbell again. She turned on her heals and walked out of the kitchen towards the door. When she reached the bottom of the stairs, she spoke through the heavy wooden door.

"What do you want Jamir?"

"I want to talk to you."

"About what?"

"About what happened. Open up."

"No. Go home to your wife."

"Riley baby. There is no wife. I know that you're not believing her. Open the door please. It's chilly out here."

Riley slowly reached for the door handle, turned the lock, and opened the door.

"Damn look at your eye." Jamir shook his head as he stepped into the hallway.

"Yea look at it." Riley said sassily. "It was worse than this."

"I'm sorry baby."

"For what? Lying to me? Or for you wife beating me up?"

"Baby I never lied to you. I'm sorry for what happened."

"So, you're saying that she is lying? What woman shows up at another woman's door for a man who isn't hers?"

"Ri, listen. That bitch is crazy. Ever since we broke up, she has been trying to ruin my life. She is pissed because I don't want to be with her anymore, so she is doing everything she can to make my life a living hell."

"I don't believe you."

"It's the truth. I put a restraining order on her."

Riley rolled her eyes. "Yea whatever."

"I'm serious."

"This is the reason you haven't wanted to commit to me, right?"

"Partially. Not because of her. I'm not with her anymore. I promise. I just haven't been wanting to move too fast into another situation. The divorce is still fresh, so I've been trying to take my time with you Riley. You've been on the fast track."

"The fast track Jamir? It has been over a year now."

"A year is not nearly a long enough time to get to know someone before committing to them."

"Are you shitting me? There are people who fall in love after a month of knowing each other. Hell, Khloe Kardashian and Lamar Odom moved faster than us and they got married."

"Baby. You're talking about celebrities."

"So, they are people. Even regular people have moved faster than us. I'm not saying we should have made it official after two or three months, but a year? You should know by now if I am the one.

"Bae. I do know. I know that you're the one."

"You're just saying that."

"No. I'm serious Ri."

Riley and Jamir shared eye contact for a second, and then he kissed her. The feeling from his thick and soft lips sent tingles through her body. She'd fallen for him again in just one kiss. Jamir pushed her up against the wall. He reached underneath Riley's dress and rubbed her peach. Jamir pulled her panties to the side and pushed his finger inside of her.

"Damn baby you missed me." he said when he felt how wet that she was.

Riley unbuttoned his jeans. He turned her around so she was facing the wall. He lifted her dress, pulled her panties off, and pushed himself inside of her. She put her hands on the wall and accepted all of him. He took her hands and held them behind her back as if he were arresting her. He held her hands and pounded into her as she leaned forward and took it. Neither one of them made a sound. The only sounds were from him pounding into her. She let out a high-pitched sigh when she got hers, and then she turned around sat down on the stairs and took him into her mouth. She sucked him clean of all her essence hungrily, and then she took his nut when he busted into her mouth. Riley hated that she missed him. She hated that she loved him. She hated that she needed him. Just like that, she was back in the middle of a love triangle.

Chapter 4

Raelyn

After my sister left the hospital, I went back into Laron's hospital room and sat in the chair next to his bed. I was still angry and shocked about the whole situation, but I was too exhausted to act on my feelings. I was just ready to get in the bathtub, get into something comfortable, and take a long nap. My sister told me to come to her house and stay for a couple of nights until things die down; just in case Paris planned to return for more. I agreed with her. I wasn't comfortable going home alone after what happened.

"Is everything ok?" Laron asked me when I sat down.

"Yea. My sister just freaked out when I told her that we were at the hospital. How are you feeling?"

"Besides feeling loopy from these pain meds, I'm alright. I'm sorry for what happened Raelyn. Seriously."

I nodded my head.

"It's over between us, huh?"

I swallowed hard. I wanted to tell him right then that I was through, but my heart would not allow me to kick a man while he was down.

"Let's not talk about that right now."

"I want to talk about it because I know that I fucked up."

"You did. You lied to me."

"I did."

"And her."

"I did, and I'm sorry. I just wasn't ready to let you go."

"Both of us could have died over this mess. I don't think you understand how scared I was."

"I know because I was too. I've never seen her like that before."

"You never know what a person is capable of when you play with their heart." I said.

"Will you forgive me?"

"I was taught to always forgive, but I will never forget. Did you contact your family?"

"I did. They will be up here soon."

"Good." I know that he could see that I was completely removed emotionally. I was just waiting for his family to show up so I could leave. I looked down at my phone to read a text message from the bouncer at my job.

"My cousin said that he will stay with me until I heal up."

"Good."

"What about the pregnancy?"

"At this point, I don't know."

"I just want you to know that I do really love you, and if you are pregnant, I will be there for you and my child."

"Thanks."

After what happened, there was no way that I was having a child by him. I said a prayer right there begging to not be pregnant. I just wanted to go to sleep and forget that any of it had ever happened. I sent a text message back to the bouncer from my job and turned my attention to the hospital room television.

Chapter 5

Riley

Jamir promised Riley that he would be more into her, and they could start working towards something more. He told her that he would stop treating her like a late-night creep. He set out to prove to her that he felt bad about the whole situation, so he started taking her out on dates instead of just showing up at her house to chill and have sex. Riley was alright with the new arrangements. She had been patiently waiting for him to come around, and he was finally showing progress.

"Why do we always chill at my place? Why haven't you invited me over to your place yet?" Riley asked.

"Because I live with roommates right now, and I don't want to bring you into a house full of men. You are too beautiful for that." Jamir responded.

"Well when do you plan to move?"

"I am working on that now. Breaking up with my ex-wife set me back a little financially, but I was tired of living with my mom, so I got a room in a house with a few guys."

Riley sighed. She wasn't sure if she believed him, but she loved him, so she didn't press the issue.

"Why are you making that face? Don't start. I'm not lying to you, and I've never lied to you. It's like since that situation went down, you've had a magnifying glass on me."

"I'm not supposed to?"

"Bae chill out."

"You're always telling me to chill out."

"Because you be doing too much sometimes. Ain't I with you?"

"Yes."

"Ain't I showing an effort to be with you?"

"Yes."

"Well, then chill Aight. I'm not hiding nothing."

"Alright. When can I introduce you to my family?"

"I'm not ready for that yet bae. In due time."

Riley pursed her lips and then she said, "Ok."

**

Riley felt her legs burning as she peddled the exercise bike at high speed. Riley noticed how quiet Raelyn was. Riley was quiet too which was not normal for either one of them. The gym was usually the time when they had most of their girl chat. Riley decided to break the silence.

"Why are you so quiet today?"

"I don't know sister. I 've just been drained since the whole situation with Laron."

"I understand, but he played you. Why dwell on it?"

"I know, but I had feelings for him. Then, to see him get shot by his wife. That was a crazy and scary experience. I still have nightmares about it. Thanks for helping me move by the way."

"You don't have to thank me. You should thank Eazy. He did most of the work, and that was over a month ago sis."

"I know. I am trying to get over it all."

"Eventually you will. Have you talked to him?"

"No. He's been calling me, but I won't answer. It is so hard to not talk to him. Some days I really miss him. I know it sounds stupid, but it's true. I wish that I never got involved in the whole crazy mess. I'm glad that I wasn't pregnant."

"What? You thought you were pregnant? Why didn't you tell me sister?"

"Because I felt stupid after the shooting and I didn't want to talk about it."

"But I'm your twin." Riley said as she pressed stop on the machine. Raelyn pressed stop on her machine too, and then they stood up and walked over to the leg machines.

"I knew that you were going to be mad." Raelyn said as she sat down. She set the weight and began lifting her legs in an upward motion.

"I am! How could you hold that back from me?" Riley asked, and then she nudged her shoulder before sitting down at the machine next to the one Raelyn was using. Riley set her weight and began squeezing her legs together.

"Well, I'm not, so there is no need to trip about it now."

"Are you going to start dating again?" she asked.

"I don't know if I am ready."

"Yea, but you can't give up like that. I hope you don't go back to your vibrator life."

"Shut up."

"What about the bouncer at work?"

"He's a nice guy, I'm really not that into him."

"Maybe because you haven't given him chance. You were too wrapped up in Laron."

"You have a point. Anyways. What's up with you? You've been distant these days. I know that you're not messing with Jamir again?"

Riley looked down at the floor.

"Sister!"

"What?"

"Why? You know he isn't any good."

"I don't know what it is about him sister. He apologized for what happened and he told me that he wanted to work towards something permanent."

"He's married."

"No, he's not. His ex-wife is just tripping because he is moving on."

"And you're believing his lies?" Raelyn asked. She took ten second break and then started a new set of leg lifts.

"Rae, I love him, and I know he loves me. We are working it out."

"I can't. I really can't. Do you hear yourself, right now? Do you think a chick is really going to show out for a dude that ain't hers?" I asked.

"Jamir doesn't want her. That bitch is delusional." Riley said, and then she paused before starting another set.

"Are you sure that you're not?" Raelyn asked.

"Whatever. She just better back off my man. He ain't hers anymore. He's mine." Riley said.

Raelyn gave her sister a stare that said that she was tripping, and then Riley said, "Anyways, you know Aleyah and her husband moved back into town."

"Oh my God when?"

"Yesterday. Mom told me. We should link up with her for lunch."

"I can't wait to see her. It has been too many years. Maybe she'll want to come out with us for our birthday." Riley said.

"I am sure she will." I said.

"She will be the reason to take your mind off Laron." she said.

Chapter 6

Paris

They had finally let me out of the mental institution and back into the world. Although I was mentally preparing to go to prison for what I did, I was happy that I got off easy. I didn't know how I got away with it, but I was not complaining. I found out later that Laron didn't press charges, so I ended up in the nut house for forty-five days. While I was in, I had my best friend and her husband go and get some of my things from Laron. He put up a fuss. He told them that they weren't getting shit, but he gave in after talking to my mom and gave them most of my things. After that, he started asking my mom if she could get me to talk to him. I refused to talk to him. I had nothing to say to him. There was no going back from what happened. He betrayed me and that was the end for me. I planned to stay with my best-friend until the divorce was final, and then I was going to move back home to California.

"Glad to see you back!" Priscilla said after she jumped out of her truck to greet me. She ran to hug me.

"I missed you girl!"

"I missed you too."

"Come on." Priscilla said. She opened the car door for me and then she got in on the driver's side.

"Girl your crazy ass could have been gone for life." she said after she closed the door.

We clicked our seatbelts, and then I said, "I know."

"What the hell were you thinking?" she asked.

"I wasn't. I swear I left my brain at home. All I knew was he had me fucked up. I temporarily lost my mind for real."

"I still can't believe you shot him."

"Girl I was so mad after he bold faced lied to me at dinner, and then he had the nerve to go to her house after he made love to me. After he lied to my face again, and told me that he was going to the airport. I was capable of doing anything that night. He better be glad that I didn't shoot his dick off like I planned to."

"Oh my gosh." Priscilla said.

"I'm over it now."

"Good because I don't need you to be locked up ever again for doing something crazy."

"I don't ever want to be locked up again. That mess was crazy. I am too pretty for that. Look at my hair and nails. They are a mess."

"You know that I am going to get you to the salon asap."

"Thanks." I gazed out the window at all the trees. Everything looked greener than before. Thoughts of that night crossed my mind. I shook my head, and then Priscilla asked, "So, what happened with the chick?"

"I don't know. I feel bad about her because she didn't know."

"Seriously? Do you believe that? That chick was trying to steal your man."

"I thought so too, but I thought about it long and hard while I was in the nut house. You should have seen the look in her eyes. It's crazy, but she seemed as shocked about me as I was about her."

"Or was she just too shocked to see a gun and a crazy woman in her house?"

I laughed. "That too, but something in her eyes told me that she was telling the truth. I've been thinking about apologizing to her."

"For what?"

"To clear my conscious. In that brief moment of insanity, I could have killed them both. I don't ever want to feel that way again."

"I say just leave it alone." she said as she pulled into the driveway of her home.

"I hear you." I said.

"Thank you." she said.

Chapter 7

Raelyn

"Sister!" Riley and I exclaimed when we walked into the restaurant and saw Aleyah sitting at one of the tables waiting for us.

"Twins!" she said excitedly when she spotted us. She stood up to hug us.

"Girl you look good!" Riley said.

I looked her over. She was still the short, brown skin, beauty that I remembered. We are all the same height, same golden-brown complexion, same facial features. People always mistake her as our triplet. We constantly tell her that she is our sister that we lost in the womb. We met in church. Our parents are best friends. We used to do everything together. We went to the same schools, and our families did birthdays and holidays together. Back in the days, Aleyah and our brother Eazy had a crush on each other, but it never went anywhere. She got married and our brother had a baby with someone else.

Aleyah said, "You two look good too! Oh my gosh. You must stay in the gym."

I said, "We do."

"It looks good on both of you." she said.

"Thanks." Riley and I said in unison.

Riley said, "It has been too long girl. We haven't seen you in five years. How have you been?"

"I've been amazing."

"That's good. Welcome back home." Riley said.

"Thank you. It feels good to be back."

"What made you move back from Atlanta after five years?"

"My husband got a better paying job up here, so we decided to come where the money is."

I said, "That makes a lot of sense."

"How is your husband and your son?" Riley asked.

"They are good. I don't know how either of them are going to get adjusted to the brutally cold winters. My husband might readjust a little faster, but my son has never seen a Minnesota winter."

"That's right. You had him while living in Atlanta. How old is he now? Five?"

"Yes."

"He'll adjust." Riley said.

"I hope so because I'm ready for it. I like the winter."

"Girl what black person likes winter?" Riley asked. All of us laughed and then she said, "Me."

"You are just as weird and you were when we were kids." I said.

She laughed. "Whatever. So, what's going on up here? I'm ready to leave my men at home and have a little fun."

"Well, you know our birthday is coming, so we are going out. We were hoping that you would be down to come out with us?"

"Oh, hell yes! My husband will have no problem keeping our little one while I get out and get some girls time."

"Cool! It's this weekend." I said.

She asked, "Do you two still bartend?"

"Yup." I said.

Riley said, "I'm over it though. I'm about to find another job until I finish school. I'm almost done. This is my last year."

"Hold up. You're trying to leave me? Why haven't you told me?"

"Yes sister. Because I was still making my mind up. My mind is made up now, so I told both of you at the same time. It's time to do something new."

"'Whatever. Anyways. You ready to party girl?" I asked Aleyah.

Aleyah said. "Hell yes."

***

I was sitting in the grass at the lake in my thoughts trying to force myself to forget about Laron and stop missing him. It was harder to force the thoughts about him out of my head than it was to just let the thoughts flow. I decided to try and tune thoughts about him out by listening to the water, and the kids playing at the playground nearby, and the people on the walkway behind me either walking, running, biking, or skating. I was focusing so hard on tuning Laron out of my head that I had forgot that my Shawn was sitting next to me.

"You must have a lot on your mind?" he asked.

I said, "I do."

"Do you want to talk about it?"

"Not really."

"Alright. I'm here for you, if you ever want to talk."

"Thanks."

"You look so tense. Give me your foot."

"For what?"

"So, I can help you relax."

"Not out here."

"Why?"

"Because people are watching."

"So. These people don't care. If anything, most people would be wishing that it was them getting the foot rub."

I smiled, turned towards him, and put my foot in his lap. I leaned back on my arms, closed my eyes, and let the slight breeze blow through my hair.

"See, I told you."

"You were right."

We sat there in silence for a while as he went to work on my feet. I broke the silence and asked, "Why is love so complicated?"

Shawn replied, "I don't know. I ask myself the same thing sometimes."

"Yea?"

"It's still mind boggling to me why my ex cheated on me. I did everything right for that woman. I never cheated, I was respectful, I never stayed out late unless I was at work. I made love to her every day accept her time of the month. I spoiled her. I bought her everything she wanted. I paid all the bills. I was working two jobs to provide for us. I even cooked for her, and she still cheated on me. I will never understand that."

"That is crazy."

"Good guys always finish last."

"No, they don't."

"Uh-huh. Only fuck boys get good girls."

I laughed. "Seriously. If I was out here cheating and beating on women, I wouldn't be able to keep them off me."

"Oh my gosh."

"They don't want a real man that they can go to church with and raise a family with. They want a dude that they got to bail out of jail, fight all his other baby's mom's, argue with all the time, and stay up all night trying to figure out where he is at."

"Wow."

"It's true."

"Not all women like bad boys."

"Um hum. So, why do you mess with one?"

"I don't."

"That guy I saw you talking to at the club is definitely one."

"No, he's not."

"Yes, he is. What happened with him?"

A flashback of Paris shooting Laron in my bedroom flashed through my head. I pulled my feet from out of his lap and crossed my legs in front of me.

"Everything and nothing at the same time." I said. I ran my fingers through my hair.

"You're not done with him yet."

I frowned. "Yes, I am."

"No, you're not. I can tell by the look in your eyes."

I smacked my lips and rolled my eyes.

"You haven't learned your lesson yet. That is why you got me in the friend zone." Shawn said.

"You're not in the friend zone." I said.

"Yes I am. How many times have we hung out? Numerous times and we've never gone past a kiss on the cheek. It's ok. I respect you and I am ok being your friend. I don't want to be caught up in no mess with you anyway."

I chuckled, threw some grass at him and said, "Shut up."

Chapter 8

Riley

Riley picked up her phone and answered it. "Hey baby." she said. Riley looked at her hand and started blowing the wet fingernail polish.

"Bitch I told you to stay away from my man! Why the fuck is you still calling him!?" the girl said. Riley took the phone from her ear and looked at the number. It was Jamir's number. The chick was calling her from Jamir's phone. Riley put the phone back to her ear.

"First of all, bitch that is not your man because if he was, he wouldn't have been over here last night."

"I guess you want me to beat that ass again!"

"You didn't beat my ass! You attacked me! Obviously, he ain't yours when he is always over here with me, and it's where he wants to be!"

"Best believe if you don't leave him alone, every time I see you, I'm beating that ass!"

"Yea whatever. Since that's your man, I hope my pussy taste good whenever you kiss him."

"I'ma see you hoe!"

The girl hung up the phone. Riley redialcd Jamir's number, but it went to voicemail, so she called again. Same thing. She repeatedly called him after that hoping that one of them would pick up, but nothing, so she sent a text message.

Why is she calling me from your phone!

***

Jamir never text back, but he called an hour later. Riley went off as soon as she answered the phone.

"What the fuck is going on! Why is she calling me from your phone!"

"I don't know man! Calm down!"

"No! Tell me what's going on!"

"I was visiting my kid, and I set my phone down to wash his hands. I guess she took my phone then."

"You're a liar Jamir!"

"I swear I wasn't on no bullshit! Look, I'm on the way. I'll talk to you when I get there."

Riley plopped down on the couch, folded her arms and started shaking her foot. Her irritation level was at an all-time high. Riley knew that he wasn't telling the truth. She couldn't understand why it took him so long to call back, or why he waited until he was in the car driving to call her back. She didn't move from the couch until she heard her doorbell ringing. She slowly walked down the wooden stairs to let him in. She barely hugged him when he stepped inside. He felt her attitude and snapped at her.

"Aye, don't start that shit, aight? I already told you what it was." he said. Riley turned and started walking back up the stairs with her arms folded across her chest. He followed her up the stairs and into the apartment. Riley closed and locked the door, and then she asked, "Then what took you so long to call me back?"

"I already told you that I was visiting with my son." he said.

"I know that you saw my text message."

"I didn't have my phone! It was on the coffee table!"

"I've never seen you without your phone when you are over here."

"My son had me distracted!"

"Yea, right!"

"I'm not about to do this back and forth with you! Come here and be quiet." He yanked Riley to him and covered her lips with his.

"Stop!" Riley yelled while trying to push him off. He gripped her tighter. He kept kissing her as he held her tight enough to keep her from moving. He kept kissing her until she gave in and allowed him to walk her to the couch. Once she laid down, he snatched her shorts off, pulled down her panties, pulled out his manhood and put himself inside of her. He dove deep inside of her and gave her aggressive thrusts until she started saying his name, and then he put her legs on his shoulders and dove deeper until she released her waterfall onto him, and then he flipped her over and back stroked her until he got tired, pulled out, and released on her.

Chapter 9

Paris

I was staring at Laron from across the conference room table. Lawyers were sitting to the side of both of us discussing the keeps and takes of our divorce. When we married, I never thought that our love story would end up like that. Divorce was not in the plans. I planned to be with Laron forever. I thought bringing another woman into the bedroom would keep our love strong. I had to find out the hard way that, that was not true.

"Can I please talk to my wife alone for a second?" Laron asked.

"No sir-" My lawyer started to speak, but I cut him off.

I said, "I'm ok. It's ok."

The lawyers excused themselves and left me and Laron in the conference room alone. Laron gave me the saddest look and asked, "Are you really going to do this?"

"Yes. I am."

"Paris, you know that I love you and I never meant to hurt you."

"But, you did."

"What about what you did to me Paris? You know I saved your ass. You could have been in prison right now."

"I've already apologized to you for what I did, and I've already thanked you for lying to the judge on my behalf."

"What if you would have killed me babe?"

"That is something that I would have had to live with and regret for the rest of my life."

"Wow."

"The amount of hurt I felt when I found out that you were going behind my back you will never understand. I've loved you wholeheartedly Laron; to the point that I would do anything for you. That was the reason we invited another woman into our bedroom. I will never be able to forgive you for lying to me."

"Baby listen, all marriages go through shit. This is minor compared to what some people go through. I made a mistake that I will never make again. I promise."

"Laron, you hurt me in the worse way. Especially when I was open to do things that I would never do. I'm done with this marriage. You will never get the chance to hurt me again."

"Can I get a hug."

"No."

"I'm coming anyway." Laron said. He stood up and then the lawyers knocked on the door. They cracked the door a little and peeped their heads in.

"Are you two, ready?" my lawyer asked.

I said, "Yes."

Laron sat down. The Lawyers took their seats again and continued with our meeting. Laron looked broken like he had just lost his best-friend. I was sitting poised and pretty like a queen. I was not backing down. His pretty eyes and sexy lips weren't going to make me weak ever again.

Triangles 3

Chapter 10

Raelyn

I ignored another call from an unsaved number. I figured it was Laron calling me from another phone because I'd blocked his number. I was in my bedroom getting dressed for me and Riley's birthday party. Our brother Eazy was hosting an event for us at one of the popular clubs downtown Minneapolis. Riley was in my bathroom getting ready. We decided to wear the same hairstyle and similar outfits. Riley was wearing shorts with boots, and I was wearing jeans with heels. Both of us were wearing matching plaid shirts with our outfits. She wrapped hers around her waist, and I was wearing mine tied up into a crop top. Riley came out of the bathroom dancing to the Kendrick Lamar song playing from my mini speaker. It had been a while since we'd been out, so we were excited.

Riley handed me a glass of Patron over ice and then she started twerking in the mirror. I laughed, took a swallow from my glass, set the glass on the dresser, and continued applying my fake eyelashes.

"I love Kendrick Lamar."

"I do too. Is Jamir going to come out tonight?"

"I told him about it, but I don't know. He said that he is not big on clubs anymore."

"Not even for your birthday?"

"I'm not tripping if he doesn't."

I stayed silent. There was no need to spew negativity her way about Jamir because she wasn't going to listen.

"When will Aleyah be here?" I asked.

"She just text saying that she would be here any minute." Riley said.

"We're going to have a ball. You know our brother Eazy."

"Yes. He has to do it big." Riley said and then my buzzer rang.

"There goes Aleyah. Buzz her in." I said. Riley danced over the door and pressed the buzzer to unlock the outside doors to the building. She opened the door and stood there to wait for Aleyah.

I heard Aleyah say, "Hey!" I walked out of my room to greet her. Aleyah walked up, reached out to hug Riley, and then walked into the apartment and gave me a hug.

"Y'all look nice! I see your twinning tonight."

"Thank you." we said in unison.

"You're looking good too sister." I said.

"Thank you. Where are the rest of the ladies?"

"They will be here any minute. Would you like a drink?" I asked.

"Yes." Aleyah said.

Riley made her a drink while I finished up my make-up. Taji and Cherry showed up a few minutes later, and then we made our way out to the limo and headed to the club.

***

"Mask Off," by Future was blaring through the speakers. We were on the dance floor screaming the lyrics at the top of our lungs with the rest of the club. We could see our brother and his crew dancing and singing the lyrics in our VIP section. I didn't know about everyone else, but me and Riley were tipsy for real. After the song ended, the five of us started walking back towards the VIP section so we could drink and party with our brother Eazy. Riley was leading the pack, Taji and Cherry were behind her, and I was behind them giggling with Aleyah about some of the people in there. I saw my sister stop short. She started having some words with some other girl, so I made my way to the front of the group. I could hear the girl yelling about how my sister was a stupid ass bitch, and how my sister needed stay away from her man. Then, my sister starting yelling back saying that the girl needed to get up out of her face. When I got to my sister, I told the chick to back up. Some guy stepped in between us to try to cool the situation down and then all hell broke loose.

The chick reached around the dude and punched my sister in the head. My sister started swinging and then I started swinging. We had her by her hair and then her friend jumped in. Next thing I knew, all of us were fighting. Eazy rushed out of the VIP section to help break it up.

Security rushed over to help break up the fight too. Weaves were pulled out, nails were broken, and the chick I was fighting shirt had ripped off. Our brother had to calm us down and make all five of us get back into the limo and leave. My hair was ruined and my outfit was damaged because of my sister's bullshit. Our birthday celebration was officially over.

"What the hell was that mess Riley!?" I yelled once the limo driver pulled off.

"That's Jamir's ex-wife. That stupid bitch."

"I've never had a fight in my life and you got me in the club fighting for you because of some stupid ass dude?!"

"That bitch had me messed up from jump. She had it coming to her."

"Did it ever occur to you that maybe if you weren't messing with that dude none of this would be happening? Riley, we don't fight! We certainly don't fight bitches in the club over no dudes."

"I know. I'm sorry sister."

I shook my head. I spoke to the other ladies. "I'm sorry ladies."

Taji said, "It's ok. I wasn't going to let those bitches jump y'all."

"Me either." Aleyah agreed.

"Thanks for having my back y'all." Riley said.

Cherry said, "No problem girl."

"I'm sorry sister."

"I don't want to hear it Riley. You need to leave that dude alone."

The rest of the ride was dead silent all the way back to my apartment.

Chapter 11

Aleyah

Aleyah walked in her house and hung her keys on her key hanger. Her husband Lamar looked up from the television. Lamar is tall, slender, and brown skin. He had on his pajama pants and a wife beater t-shirt with a pair of house shoes on his feet.

"What are doing home so early?" Lamar asked.

Aleyah said, "Man baby. Tonight, was wild. The twins got into a huge fight and the rest of us wound up in it." She took her heels off and put them on the mat by the door. She walked over to the couch and sat down next to her husband.

"What the hell? Are you ok?"

"Yes. It was bad, but I am ok. I only broke a nail. The girls we were fighting got tore up though."

"What happened?"

"I don't know. We were having fun. We started walking. I heard some yelling. They started swinging and the next thing I knew, we were all fighting. Their brother and security broke it up."

"What the hell baby? Fighting? You haven't had a fight in years."

"I know. I wonder if somebody recorded it because I was tapping that ass."

Lamar chuckled a little. "You're crazy. Something serious could have happened."

"I know. I'm glad it didn't. I can't believe I still got hands though. I thought I lost it."

Lamar laughed again and then he asked, "What was the fight over?"

"The twins were arguing in the limo on the way back. Sounds like it was over some dude."

"Ah hell naw baby. The twins fighting over a dude?"

"I know. I said the same thing. I would never fight a chick over a dude, but if she disrespects me, she can get these hands."

"Sounds like the twins have changed. I've never known them to fight."

"They have, but we all have since our church days."

"Not you. You're still wild and crazy."

"Be quiet. No one in church knew that I was wild and crazy, and I have calmed down a lot since we had our son."

"I will agree with that. I'm just glad you're ok and nothing crazy happened to any of y'all." Lamar said.

Aleyah smiled. She liked how calm her husband Lamar was. He was the best at diffusing a situation. If he was there at the club with them, the fight would have probably never happened. He is a quiet, chill type of person. He enjoys a good party, but he isn't the life of the party. Aleyah is a loud, wild, life of the party, socialite kind of girl. He was the calm to her storm in most situations.

"I am too. Anyways. Where is little man?"

"Sleep."

"I was thinking the whole way home."

"About what?"

"About getting home to my chocolate bar."

"Oh, were you?" he smiled.

"Yes." Aleyah giggled and touched the crouch of Lamar's pajama pants. When she felt the bulge, she smiled. She slid off her panties while he took his pajama pants and underwear off. She climbed on top of him and put his thickness inside of her. She began bouncing on him.

"I love when you come home like this baby." Lamar said as he watched his wife give it to him. It was feeling good to him, so he flipped her over onto her back and got on top of her. Aleyah wrapped her legs around him and started telling him how good it was, and then right when she started to get lost in the feeling, her husband lost himself and busted.

"Ugh shit baby." he groaned as he released himself.

Aleyah watched him get his while trying hard not to roll her eyes. It was nothing new for him to bust fast. He always busted quick unless he had been drinking. That seemed to be the only time that he could control it. It was something that she had accepted about him over the years, and his head game would make up for it most times. Lamar kissed her and told her that he loved her. She replied the same.

"Babe. Can I get a round two tonight?" she asked.

"Baby we both have to get up early in the morning"

"So."

"Babe I got to get my rest or else I will be no good at work."

Aleyah sighed and said, "Ok."

They stood up and headed to the bedroom to go to bed.

Chapter 12

Riley

Raelyn's door buzzer blaring through the apartment woke Riley up. She was lying on the couch at her sister's apartment. She opened her eyes, pulled herself off the couch, and dragged herself to the door. She knew it was their brother Eazy coming to go off on them both for the shenanigans they pulled at their party the night before. He had text messaged both sisters telling them that he would be over there in the morning. Riley knew that it was all her fault, but she wasn't in the mood to hear it. She had a bad hangover and her head was pounding.

Who is it? she said into the loud speaker

"Me." she heard Eazy's voice respond, so she pressed the button to buzz him in.

Raelyn heard the buzzer and dragged herself out of bed. She walked out of the bedroom to the living room.

"Who was it?"

"Eazy."

"Oh boy."

"I know."

"It's your fault."

"I know."

Eazy knocked on the door and then walked in fuming looking like a younger version of their father. Brown skinned, muscular, dressed in a white muscle t-shirt, and grey sweatpants.

"What the fuck was that shit last night twins!?" he asked angrily.

Riley said, "Eazy calm down."

Raelyn threw her hands up. "I had nothing to do with it."

"The bitch stepped to me." Riley said.

"I heard her yelling something about her man. Are you fucking with someone else's dude?"

"No."

"Yes, she is." Raelyn said.

"He isn't with her anymore."

"You're fighting over dudes now!? Come on Ri!"

"That is what I said." Raelyn said.

"You were taught better than that. You haven't even brought dude around the family, so he can't be that special."

"I planned to."

"Not if you're fighting his other chicks Riley!" he yelled.

"Calm down."

"I'm just saying. That shit ain't cool."

Raelyn shook her head. "That's what I said." she said.

Riley folded her arms and said, "I'm sorry."

"Sorry ain't gonna cut it. You had everybody up in that shit. You don't fight and neither does Rae. You had Aleyah fighting and she just got back up here. I didn't even get a chance to chill with her. I could have lost my business with the owner over that shit." Eazy said.

"Well, I said sorry. I don't know what else to say."

Eazy said, "You need to be done fucking with that dude for real."

"For real sis." Raelyn said.

"Whatever." Riley said.

"Whatever? Ok twin. I am about to go." Eazy said. "I'll hit you later Rae." He turned and walked out of the door.

***

"I got into a fight with your ex-wife last night at the club." Riley said into the phone.

"Huh? How the hell did that happen?"

"She must have spotted me, so she rolled up on me with her crew. Some words were exchanged and she threw the first punch."

"Oh man. I 'm sorry."

"I can't understand why she keeps attacking me, if y'all are no longer together."

"Because she is crazy as hell. That's why I'm not with her. She be on that bullshit. Don't worry. I'm gonna check her ass."

"Now, my family is mad at me. I'm not going to be fighting chicks over you Jamir. I wish you could have been there."

"Bae, I'm sorry. I will be over there tomorrow. I am going to put a stop to this bullshit."

"Ok. I love you."

"Aight, talk to you later."

Riley looked at the phone. She watched him end the call without telling her that he loved her back once again.

Chapter 13

Raelyn

I ignored another call from an unsaved number, and took a bite of food.

"How the hell did y'all end up fighting at the club?" Shawn asked.

"It was my sister's fault. She was arguing with some chick over her dude." I said.

"Oh wow. I was at the bar, and I looked over and all I saw was arms swinging and weaves flying." Shawn said.

I chuckled and took another bite of food.

"I didn't know y'all had a little hood in y'all."

I laughed. "Shut up. I was defending my sister. Our brother was pissed though."

"I know he was. I tried to call you to make sure that you and sister were ok, but you didn't answer."

"My phone died and I was too drunk to care. I put it on the charger and passed out. I'm sorry. Thanks for this birthday lunch by the way."

"Anything for you beautiful." he said with a smile. My mind went straight to thoughts of Laron, but I smiled back and said, "Thank you."

"I love looking at you. Everything about you is beautiful to me." he said.

I know that he was being sweet, and I appreciated it, but I wasn't receiving it how I should have been because my mind was on Laron. I changed the subject.

"You're too sweet. Um, what time is it. I need to get out of here soon. That's right. You're hooking up with your sister and your God-sister at the gym."

"Yup."

"Ok let me get you out of here. By the way, I would love to work out with you sometime. I've been trying to get back on some healthy living type stuff and get back into shape."

"Sure, I'm down, so just let me know."

"I will."

Shawn paid for the bill, walked me to my car, opened my car door for me, and said goodbye. I still hadn't so much as kissed Shawn since hanging out with him. I was starting to see what he meant by being stuck in the friend zone. I started my car and pulled out. I took a right turn onto Lake Street and then a left turn when I reached Hennepin Avenue. I decided to answer the call coming from the unsaved number.

"Hello?"

"It's about time you answered." Laron said.

"Did it occur to you that I wasn't answering because I knew that it was you calling from another number?"

"I know, but I kept trying because I wanted to hear your voice. I miss you." The sound of his voice made me feel butterflies in my stomach as usual, but I didn't respond.

He asked, "How have you been? Are you ok?"

I replied, "I'm fine. You should be calling your wife to see how she is doing."

"We are not together anymore."

"Neither are we, so why are you calling?"

"I want the opportunity to right my wrongs."

"I think you should just leave things the way they are."

"You don't miss me?"

I paused. "No."

"Yes, you do."

"Whatever. I'm about to go. Bye."

I hung up, dropped the phone onto my passenger seat, and then I hit the steering wheel with my hand to let out frustration. I hated that I wanted him so bad. I craved for his touch and the sound of his voice every night. I was trying hard to fight it. I shook off the feeling and kept driving towards the gym.

***

"That mess at the club was crazy you two." Aleyah said.

"I'm sorry sissy. It was my fault, but she swung first." Riley said.

"I know. I saw her. I was like oh hell no! Boop! Boop! Boop!" She started punching the air along with her sounds affects. Riley and I laughed.

I said, "We have never had a fight in our lives. I broke two nails messing around with that chick.

Riley said, "At least you only got two broken nails. The first time, I ended up with a bald patch in the back of my head and a black eye."

Aleyah frowned and asked, "First time? This has happened before?"

"Yes. At my house. She attacked me."

"Who is this chick?" Aleyah asked.

"My boyfriend's ex-wife."

"Boyfriend? When did you gradate to that status?" I asked.

Riley rolled her eyes at me. "Well, it's a guy that I'm seeing."

Aleyah asked, "Are you sure she's his ex?"

"Yes."

"Hmmm. I don't think that I would be doing all that for my ex." Aleyah said.

I said, "I agree."

"Shut up Raelyn. Don't sit here and try to act like you don't have any drama."

I knew she was trying to deflect the attention from her, and before I could switch the conversation back on her, Aleyah said, "What? You got chicks throwing punches at you too?"

I said, "No."

"She got chicks pulling guns and shooting their man in front of her though."

"Shut up Riley." I said.

"Uh, uh. My business is out there, so I'm putting yours out there too." Riley said.

Aleyah stopped stretching, looked at me with a frown on her face, and said, "What the hell Rae?"

"It's a long story. I don't feel like talking about it. He and I are done."

"Oh my. You two have changed. I remember when I was the wild one and you two were innocent. Now, you two got me beat by a long shot. Do your parents know about this?

"Hell no, so please don't mention it around them." Riley said.

"What about Eazy?" Aleyah asked.

"Not about my situation, so please don't mention it to him either." Raelyn said.

"Speaking of Eazy, have you talked to him since you been back?" Riley asked.

"No. I saw him briefly at your birthday party." Aleyah said.

"You know he would love to talk to you and see you girl." Riley said.

"He is so in love with you." Raelyn said.

"Be quiet you guys. You know that I'm married." Aleyah said.

"You know that you broke his heart when you did that." Riley said.

"I know, but I had to do what was right. At the time, I was pregnant, and he had a baby on the way." Aleyah said.

"We would had rather you be a part of the family over that bitch that he had a baby with." Raelyn said. Aleyah laughed.

"You two were so cute back in the day being best friends and stuff." Riley said.

"We were best friends. We were too scared to mess around back then because we knew our parents would've killed us. That is how we ended up messing with other people."

"I always thought y'all did something with each other." I said.

"Me too." Riley said.

"Nope." Aleyah replied.

"Wow." I said.

"So, your husband was your first?" Riley asked.

"Not quite. There was one before him that I will not mention because he was an A.W.O.T."

"What is that?" Riley asked.

"A waste of time." Aleyah said. We laughed and then I asked, "Speaking of your husband, is he getting settled in?"

"Yup, oh and before I forget we are having some friends over for dinner tomorrow night and I would love for you two to come. I know it is short notice, and it's on Friday. Do you have to work?"

"Usually we would, but there is a private event at our job, so we have the night off. We can come."

"Oh good! I just knew that you guys were going to say no. Ok, so I am going to text you the time and my address."

Chapter 14

Aleyah

Lamar opened the door and slapped hands with his best friend Niko.

"What's up bruh!" Lamar said.

"Long time no see bruh!" Niko said.

"I know man! Come in."

"Hey Niko!" Aleyah said when he walked into their house.

"Hi beautiful." Niko said. He embraced Aleyah in a tight hug and then kissed her on the cheek. Niko has a lighter brown complexion than Aleyah and Lamar, and he is covered in tattoos. He introduced them to the girl he had with him.

"This is Faye."

"Nice to meet you." Aleyah said. "You two make yourself at home. More people should be arriving soon. Aleyah walked back into the kitchen to finish preparing dinner.

"What y'all drinking?" Lamar asked.

"You got some Cîroc?" Niko asked.

"I got you bruh. Are you good with that Miss lady?" Lamar asked Faye.

"Yes."

"Aight I'll be right back." Lamar fixed the two of them a drink, and then he sat down with them to talk and get caught up with Niko. The twins arrived shortly after Lamar sat down with Niko and Faye. Aleyah introduced everyone. A couple more of Lamar's friends showed up after the twins and then Lamar joined Aleyah in the kitchen to help her finish getting things prepared for dinner. Aleyah was in her element. She loved planning and hosting gatherings for her friends and family. Lamar kissed her on the cheek when he walked up to her.

"You look sexy tonight baby." he said.

She smiled and said, "Thank you. You know what I want later."

"Oh yea?" he asked.

"Um hum. I could do you right now." Aleyah said.

"I would let you, but I don't want to scare our guests off." Lamar said.

Aleyah laughed, and then Lamar asked what she needed help with. She gave him a beautifully colored bowl and asked him to put the salad that she made in it. As he put the salad she'd prepared in the bowl he said, "I am glad everyone could come. I know how much you love having people over."

"Me too babe. Niko looks more beefed up than I remember him." Aleyah said.

"Yea. He said that he's been hitting the gym a lot."

"I see. When did he get all those tats?"

"I don't know. Over the last five years."

"Wow."

"I know. I don't even have one."

"I know. Neither do I. He looks good though." Aleyah said.

"Hey."

"What?"

"Don't be over there lusting for my boy."

Aleyah laughed. "Shut up. Anyways. What do you think about him and Faye?"

"They look good together."

"Yea they do. I like her. She is cool."

"I like him with her. He seems happier."

"I agree."

"The twins are all grown up."

"They are, and fit."

"Um hum." he responded.

"You can't have them baby." Aleyah laughed.

Lamar chuckled. "Be quiet. They are like my little sisters."

"I know baby," she said as they both walked to put the food on the table. Aleyah told everyone to come to the table dinner table. Once everyone was seated and eating, she sparked up some conversation. The twins talked about the fight they had, and they had everyone at the table laughing until their stomachs hurt.

Niko asked everyone, "Y'all trying to go out tonight?"

"Hell yea. Mama got our little man." Aleyah said. "Are you down babe?" she asked Lamar.

"Yea. That's cool." Lamar responded.

Niko looked at the twins, "Y'all down?"

"Yea we're with it." Riley said.

Everyone one else at the table said they were with it too. Aleyah started cleaning up while the guys stepped outside to smoke. The ladies stayed inside and helped Aleyah clean the kitchen.

"You and your husband are really cute together." Faye said.

Faye's complexion is that of dark chocolate. She is tall, with wide hips, and thick thighs. She was wearing her natural curly hair in a bun on top of her head, and natural looking make-up. Her nails were short, and she smelled like vanilla and brown sugar lotion.

Aleyah said, "Thank you."

"How long have you been married?" Faye asked.

"Been together six years, and married five years." Aleyah responded.

"That is beautiful." Faye said.

"How long have you known Niko?" Aleyah asked.

"I met him in college. We've been best friends ever since." Faye said.

"Aw sweet." Faye smiled and then she looked at the twins, "I've been wanting to ask y'all who does your hair?"

"Me too. I need a stylist." Aleyah said.

"We go to Sasha's."

"I have a friend who goes there. Which stylist?"

"It's so hard to get in with Sasha, so we go to anybody." Riley said.

"Yea everyone is good in there."

"Please share the info." Faye said.

"I have her card in my purse." Riley pulled out two cards and handed them to Faye and Aleyah.

Aleyah said, "Thanks. Alright let's go. No fighting tonight twins." Everyone laughed and stood up. All the ladies met the men outside and then they headed out to the club.

***

Niko and Faye were dancing with everyone especially Aleyah and Lamar. After a few drinks, Aleyah was in her zone. She was twerking on Niko and Faye was dancing with Lamar. Riley tapped Raelyn and they both started watching. They had never seen Aleyah dancing so proactive, or Lamar dance with another woman in the manner that he was. They gave each other a side eye and went back to doing their thing. When the night was over the twins said goodbye, and went home.

Niko asked, "Do y'all want to go to another party?"

"I'm down. How about you babe?" Aleyah asked. Lamar said. "That's cool."

"Ok follow us in your car." Niko said.

"Cool." Aleyah said.

Aleyah and Lamar followed Niko and Faye through downtown Minneapolis to a Mansion by the sculpture garden on the southside of Minneapolis. They found parking on the street and walked up to the house. There were already a bunch of cars parked outside the house and up and down the street.

Niko said, "This is a friend of mine's house. He always throws private parties. It should be a good time. I've already told him that you two were coming, so he put your names on the list."

They stopped at the door to give the door man their names, and then they walked into the enormous house and followed Niko into what looked like a lounge area. People were either standing or sitting on the couches sipping drinks and talking. A few people were slightly dancing to the music playing. A tall Caucasian guy walked up to Niko. "Sup Bruh." he said. He slapped hands with Niko.

"Sup bruh. This is my boy Lamar and his wife Aleyah, and you remember Faye."

Niko's friend said, "Yes." Hey beautiful." he said to Faye. He hugged her and kissed her on the cheek and then he turned to Lamar and Aleyah and said, "Nice to meet you." He shook hands with both them, and then he spoke to all of them. "Thanks for coming. Help yourself to whatever. My only rule is; have a good time. If you need me I'll be around."

"Aight cool bruh." Niko said.

"You need party favors?" he asked Niko.

"Nah I got some bruh."

"Alright." He shook hands with Niko and Lamar again and walked off.

"Let's get some drinks." Niko said. They walked to the bar. Niko shook hands with a few other people that he knew on the way. After they had their drinks in hand, Niko pulled a small canister of mints out of his pockets and said, "Party favors?"

"Yup." Aleyah said. She took one of the small pills out of the canister and then handed one to Lamar. Faye did the same. They swallowed the pills down with their drinks.

"The real party is downstairs. Follow me. "Niko said. They followed Niko through the living room and down some stairs to another level of the house They could hear music playing louder as they got closer. The DJ was mixing a genre of rap music called trap music. "Slippery" by Migos was bumping through the speakers. Niko and Aleyah danced and rapped the lyrics to the song as they walked through the hallway. Lamar and Faye followed bouncing a little to the music as they walked. They walked through a long hallway which had a few rooms. None of the rooms had doors on them. The rooms were occupied with people doing sexual activities. That's when Aleyah and Lamar figured out what kind of party they were at.

Aleyah smiled. She and Lamar were not strangers to that kind of party. They used to attend them all the time with some friends of theirs while living in Atlanta, but it had been a while since they'd been to one. Aleyah started going to them first, and then she introduced Lamar to the lifestyle after going a few times. The first time Aleyah heard about those kinds of parties was from her co-worker/friend. Aleyah's friend told her about them and then invited her one night. Aleyah was curious to see what it was like, so she went. Aleyah enjoyed the experience, so she went a few more times with her friend. The ladies never did anything at the parties, but they just liked to go and watch, and then go home and get freaky with their husbands.

One night, Aleyah's friend and her husband invited Aleyah and Lamar to a swinger's party. Aleyah talked Lamar into going. After hanging out a few times at the parties, the couple invited them into their bedroom. Aleyah and Lamar decided to experiment, so they accepted the invite, and the two couples engaged in some intense group sex with each other. Aleyah liked it, so she talked Lamar into going to more swinger's parties, which led to them inviting other couples into their bedroom. They lived the swinger's lifestyle for a while, but then Aleyah got pregnant with their son, and then work and home life took over, so they stopped hanging out as much.

It had been a long time since they'd been in that kind of atmosphere. Aleyah was surprised that Niko was into that kind of stuff, but she was happy that he was. Some hot and freaky fun was long overdue for her and Lamar, and she was ready to get her scratch itched. The four of them stopped at each room and watched for a little bit. The first one had redbone girl taking pipe from two brown skin guys. Niko slapped hands with Lamar as they watched. The next one they stopped at had a heavyset, brown skin, guy getting head from two Caucasian girls. They watched for a while and then they kept walking until they reached the main area where the music was playing.

There were a bunch of people dancing near the DJ booth watching everything going on. It was a sprawling living room style area with several couches and chairs surrounding the room. The area was lit up with some red lights. There were a few flat screen televisions on the walls showing porn movies. The music was loud, but it wasn't so loud that they couldn't hear over it. They could hear the erotic sounds from the movies, and people doing each other around the room mixed in with the music. Aleyah looked around. She spotted a skinny brown skinned guy doing a girl doggy style up against the wall, two redbone females were on one of the couches in a sixty-nine-position giving each other head, and some Asian girl fucking the shit out of a guy on a chair in the corner. She saw a room that had a door person collecting jackets, clothes, and handing out condoms. Aleyah looked at Lamar and smiled. She knew that it was going to be a good night. She liked how the parties would make Lamar all rowdy and freaky in the bedroom. It seemed to be the only time she could get the type of loving she liked from her husband. Drunk and high on pills and around a bunch of freaky stuff going on.

Niko lit a blunt and then they blended in with all the people on the dance floor as "Swang" by Rae Sremmurd begin playing through the speakers. It didn't take long for them to start feeling the effects of the pills and the marijuana. They were in a zone and after a few songs they were standing up against a wall watching everyone else in the party. Aleyah and Lamar had been to many parties, and they were all different depending on who threw them. Some of them were straight up orgy's, some of them were classy and organized, and a few of them were house parties like the one they were at that night. Aleyah like the ones that were like house parties because they were more fun.

Aleyah saw Faye reach down and start rubbing the crotch of Niko's jeans. She loved how sexy Niko looked smoking the blunt as Faye touched him. Aleyah watched as Faye bent down in front of Niko, pulled out his manhood, and put in her mouth. Aleyah was surprised that Faye was into that lifestyle too. She watched for a minute and was more turned on by watching them then she was watching everyone else in the party. Niko passed the blunt to Lamar, and then Aleyah decided to join the party. She'd never done anything at a party like that, but she was ready for some excitement, and she knew that it would be the best time to get what she wanted from Lamar. He was high, so he would be in a zone.

Aleyah bent down in front of Lamar and took him into her mouth. She saw Niko and Lamar slap hands as they both leaned up against the wall getting pleasure from their ladies. Aleyah was putting on a show and she could feel Niko watching her. She wondered if he was as turned on by her as she was him. She sucked Lamar slow and deep, and Faye sucked Niko fast using one hand to massage him as she sucked him. Her eyes surveyed Niko's tattoo covered arms and his gangster stance as he watched Faye go to work on his manhood. She tried not to stare too long, so she turned her eyes back to her husband who had his head leaned back on the wall and his eyes closed. She saw Niko tell Faye to stand up and then he bent her over against the wall, pulled her dress up over her butt, and put his manhood into her.

Aleyah stood up and Lamar picked her up and put her up against the wall. She hiked her dress up and wrapped her legs around him. He pulled her panties to the side and entered her, and then she started bouncing on Lamar. Lamar buried his face in her neck as he pounded into her. As her husband gave her the business, she couldn't keep her eyes off Niko giving Faye the business.

There was something about Niko that turned her on more than any other guy she'd seen having sex. She started thinking about what Niko would feel like inside of her and her peach got wetter. She started to moan louder which made Lamar go harder, and then she reached her peak. She dug her nails into his back as her orgasm rocked her, and then she heard Faye moaning loudly next to her. She felt Niko's eyes on her again, so she looked at him again. They locked eyes for a moment and then Niko lost himself. He pulled out of Faye and busted on her back. Aleyah looked away from him, but she was so turned on by him that she reached her peak again, and then she felt her Lamar lose it. He groaned pulled out and busted into his hand. Aleyah put her feet back onto the floor and smiled at him. He started laughing and kissed her. Niko handed Lamar one of the white rags he had in his back pocket. After they were finished, they followed Niko to one of the bathrooms where there were packages of new towels to get cleaned up. The ladies went into one bathroom and the fellas went into the other and then they all met in the hallway.

"Y'all want to go get some breakfast?" Niko asked.

"Hell yea. I'm starving." Aleyah said. "What about you baby?"

"Yup." Lamar said.

"Alright cool." Niko said.

The four of them left the party and headed to a breakfast spot Uptown. It was daylight when they emerged from the house. When Aleyah and Lamar made it home they made love again until mid-afternoon, and then they slept until Aleyah's mom dropped off their son.

Chapter 15

Riley

Riley picked up her phone and answered a call from an unsaved number. "Bitch quit calling my phone!" Riley yelled into the phone. The female on the other end giggled and then hung up the phone. Riley knew that it was Jamir's ex-wife before she answered the phone. Kiesha had been calling Riley from random numbers taunting and threating her for weeks after the fight at the club. Riley was getting fed up with it all. She had started to think that her sister was right. No woman would be going that hard for a man that isn't hers. Just then, Jamir had walked in the door. She'd left the door open for him when he told her that he was on the way. They'd plan to watch the latest episode of a television series called "Power". Riley was standing in her kitchen pouring popcorn into a bowl.

"Why the hell does your ex keep calling me and playing on my phone?"

"When did she call?"

"Just now. She laughed and hung up. I am getting sick of the childish bullshit with her."

"I don't know why she is doing all that. I told you that she is crazy."

Riley stayed quiet for a second while putting ice into a couple of glasses for them. She turned to face him, crossed her arms in front of her, and asked, "Jamir, are you sure that you're not still messing with her?"

"No bae. I'm not dealing with her crazy ass, and for that reason. If it wasn't for my son, I wouldn't be dealing with her at all. Real talk. Just block the number."

"She is calling from different numbers."

"Change your number."

"I shouldn't have to change my number because your ex can't get some act right. I'm just saying. Women don't act like that for nothing. There has to be more than what you've been telling me."

Jamir touched her face gently. "Bae. I promise. There is nothing more ok?"

Riley nervously sang, "Ok." She turned back to the two glasses and mixed vodka and cranberry juice in them. Jamir grabbed the bowl of popcorn, and Riley picked up the two glasses. She followed Jamir to her couch and sat down.

"Do you love me Jamir?" she asked.

"Here you go. Bae, you already know how I feel about you."

"No, I don't. That's why I'm asking. When are we going to be together?"

"We are together."

"As in, I am your woman and you are my man."

"Here you go with those titles. You know I don't like titles. Why can't we be without all that extra? We are fine. We both know that we both care deeply for each other, so let's leave it like that."

"Yea, but, we are not official."

"Ri, ain't I here ninety percent of the time?"

"Yes."

"Ok then, why are you tripping? When do I have time to entertain any other woman besides you?"

Riley stared into his eyes. He pulled her chin to him and kissed her on the lips. She exhaled, picked up the remote, and turned the television up.

***

Before the television show had ended, Jamir had Riley's legs spread East and West with his face in her middle eating her cupcake like it was the best frosting he'd ever tasted. He was licking, slurping, and sucking on her pearl. Her toes were curled, and she was squeezing the couch with her hands, winding her hips in a circle, and moaning his name.

"Ahh. Ja-mir-righ-there." she moaned as he was taking her to other planets with his tongue. She froze and curled her toes back up when she felt that O.

"Ah! Riley screamed and started moving backwards to get away from him.

"Uh-uh." Jamir said. He pulled her to him and continued to work on her pearl. Riley screeched and grabbed his head.

"Ah shit. Oh my. Mmm shit." she moaned. She hit a high note and then she reached her peak and creamed.

"Damn baby. Look at that shit." he smiled, stood up, and removed his boxers. She looked over his brown skin and tattoos. She wanted him bad. She stood up, wrapped her arms around him and began kissing him feverishly. He picked her up, and then she wrapped her legs around him. Jamir held her by her ass and inserted himself into her wet center. She slid down on him and began bouncing and grinding on him as he walked with her to the bedroom. He stopped walking when he stepped into the bedroom and put her up against the wall. He pounded into her up against the wall and then he put her on her dresser. He continued to give it to her on the edge of her dresser. She was biting her bottom lip and Jamir was sucking on her neck. He picked her back up and carried her to the bed. He laid her on her back and started grinding circles into her, and then he pushed her legs to the ceiling and dug into her deep.

"Oooo, shit, Ja-mir." she moaned as he gave her deep aggressive thrusts. Riley grabbed her breasts and began rubbing her nipples with her thumb and first finger, and then she put one of her nipples into her mouth. She sucked on her nipple while looking Jamir in the eyes. That turned Jamir on even more.

"Oh, that's what you on?"

"Um hum."

"You wanna catch this nut?"

"Um hum."

"Aight."

He pulled out of her and stood over her face and begin rubbing himself slowly. She opened her mouth for him. He continued to rub himself until he busted into her mouth. He grunted when he released himself. He kept rubbing until it was all out of him. She took it and drank every, last, drop. She licked her lips and smiled at him

He chuckled a little and said, "Girl you nasty."

"Only for you, bae."

"Yea that kind of shit will make a dude never go anywhere."

"Are you saying if I keep doing that, you will give us a title?"

"Bae stop it." Riley rolled her eyes.

"Come lay with me. I need to bounce earlier than usual. I have a flight to catch."

"What time?"

"I gotta bounce around one o'clock in the morning." he said. Riley sucked her teeth. "Chill. You know that I am coming right back to you." Jamir said.

"I was thinking. You should leave some stuff here, so you don't always have to stop at home first before coming over here. I also got a key for you.

"What"

"Yea. I had it made the other day."

Riley reached into her night stand and pulled out a key on a key ring that had the number fifteen on it.

"What is the fifteen for?"

"That is the year we got back together."

"That was thoughtful Ri, for real."

"Jamir. I want to be with you. I want us to be together in a real relationship. We are perfect for each other. I am ready to introduce you to my family. Especially my parents, and I want to be your wife and have a family."

"I hear you, bae. In due time, but not right now."

"When? When will you be ready?"

"Here you go again with the drama. All the time." Jamir said.

Riley exhaled loudly. "I have things on my mind that I want to talk about. I have questions that I need answers to." she said.

"Yea, but you be killing the vibe sometime with all that. Just chill."

"Bae."

"Shhhh."

"Bae."

He put his finger over her lips to quiet her. Riley backed down.

Chapter 16

Raelyn

I was drying the rest of the glasses that the bar back had just finished washing so I could put them away and leave work for the night. Riley was doing the same. Shawn walked up to the bar and spoke to us.

"Y'all tryna go get some breakfast?" he asked.

"Yea I am starving." I said.

"Nah, I'm exhausted. I am going to get home. I have a test in the morning."

"Damn Riley this is your last two weeks with us huh?" Shawn asked.

"Yup. I can't wait to start my new job."

I instantly felt sad. "So, you really don't care that you are leaving me Ri?" I felt tears forming in my eyes, but I held them back.

"You know I care sister. I love you." She walked up to me and hugged me.

"I love you too." I said.

"Aww you two are too cute." he said. We laughed, and then I hung a wine glass. I tossed the white towel that I used to dry the glasses in a bin of dirty towels. The owner handles the laundry every day, so we were done for the night. I double checked the bar to make sure everything was clean before leaving.

"Well I guess it's just me and you Raelyn." Shawn said.

"Yup." I said as he followed me and Riley out of the door. I gave my sister a hug and then I got in to my car. As I followed him down Hennepin Avenue towards Uptown, Laron called my phone. He was calling from a different number again.

"Hello?"

"Hey Rae."

"Why are you calling me so late?"

"You know that I know what time you get off work."

"Anyways. What do you want?"

"I want to see you."

"La-" He cut me off.

"Before you get ready to say no, hear me out. Why would I keep calling you, if I didn't care? If it was just about a fuck, I would be on to the next. I am a single man right now. I know that I omitted some of the truth, but I love you for real and I want to see you. I miss you baby."

"You lied, and almost got us both killed."

"Ok. I lied baby and I am sorry."

"You've already apologized. You don't have to do it again."

"Can we at least talk? Give me that. I can meet you somewhere."

"No."

"Where you at?"

"On my way to get something to eat."

"With that buster ass dude, you were with?"

"Excuse me? How do you know I am with someone? Are you stalking me?"

"No. I stopped by the club tonight to try to catch you, and I saw you leaving with him."

"Don't do that. Don't come by my job Laron."

"Alright I won't do it again, if you agree to meet with me."

I sighed. "Persistence has always been your strength."

"You gotta go for what you want, so how long are you going to be with him? Like an hour?"

"Yea."

"Meet me at the coffee shop up the street from your house in an hour and a half."

"Fine."

I hung up the phone and scratched my scalp. I didn't know why I'd agreed to meet up with him when I knew that I was weak for him. I told myself that I would just have to stand strong against temptation, although temptation had already won half the battle when I agreed to meet up with him. I told myself that my mind was stronger than my flesh and that I was not weak. I could handle a quick conversation with Laron. I pulled into the greasy spoon restaurant and parked my car next to Shawn's. I got out of the car and followed him into the restaurant.

"You look exhausted Raelyn."

"I am."

"You should come by my place. I could give you a back massage."

I gave him a skeptical look and twisted my lips up.

He chuckled. "What?"

"A back massage? Stop playing."

He laughed some more. "Naw nothing sexual Rae. My momma taught me to respect women. I would never use a back massage to get some. Damn that's how you see a brotha? I've accepted that I am in the friend zone, but damn you see me as that kind of corny?"

"I'm just saying."

"Rae, if that was the case, I would have *been* trying to get those panties off. I've been hanging out with you and talking to you all this time because I like you. Not just to hit it. I just wish you saw in me what I see in you, and what I see in us. We could be something great, but you won't give us a chance. Partially because I'm not your type, and the other part is because you are still stuck on old boy."

"How do you figure you're not my type?"

"Come on Rae. I see you talking to the kind of guys you like in the club all the time. You like the pretty boys with muscles. I am just a chubby dude."

"Whatever you're completely wrong"

"I'm right. Just like the dude you stuck on."

"You are not right. I like all kind of guys." I was lying. He was right. I do like pretty boys, but I didn't want to hurt his feelings.

"Ok Rae. Anyways. When are we going to work out together?"

"Whenever you're ready."

"I've been ready."

"What do you do during the week."

"I work."

"As a bouncer?"

"Naw Rae. I have another job."

"What? I never knew that. What do you do?"

"I'm the director of a youth program at the community center."

"Seriously?"

"Yea. I have a degree and I decided to stay in the community to make a difference. Especially with our at-risk youth. We have basketball, dance, art, music and more. It keeps them off the streets and out of trouble. I love children, and I love to see them thrive and be all they can be. It's been hard keeping it going with the government cutting a lot of funding for programs like mine, but I've kept it pushing. We hold fundraisers to get people in the community involved, so we can continue to give our kids what they need."

"Wow. That is impressive."

"You should come through sometime and check it out. The kids would love to meet you."

"Ok. I will."

"Cool. Thanks for coming to get breakfast with me."

"No problem."

***

My heart was beating rapidly as I pulled my car into the Dunn Brothers coffee shop parking lot. It was close to six o'clock in the morning. The sun was up and I was tired. Usually by that time I would have been in bed passed out sleep after a vibrator induced orgasm. I was still fantasizing about Laron, even though I knew he wasn't any good for me.

I took a few deep breaths to slow my heart rate, and then I rehearsed the plan in my head. *Hear what he needs to say, and then leave before it gets too deep.* I thought.

"Ok, I got this." I said out loud. I got out of the car, locked the doors with my key ring, and walked to the door of the coffee shop. I could see him sitting in one of the booths waiting for me as I made my way through the first glass door. He was wearing a black shirt, and jeans. He had a pair of clear glasses on his face. I was surprised to see that he'd cut his dreads off and was rocking a faded haircut with waves at the top. He looked extremely good to me. I knew right then that I wasn't going to past the test, but I was going to put in a hardcore effort to try. After I walked through the second glass door, I made my way over to him. He stood up to greet me with a smile on his face.

"Hey Rae." he said as he hugged me.

When I caught a whiff of his cologne, I knew that it was going to be more than a challenge to keep myself together. I could feel my kitty talking to me, and she was speaking loudly. I felt the thumping in my panties and I started checking myself mentally. *I don't know why I decided to do this. Rae keep it together girl.* I said to myself. I kept a straight face when I spoke back. "What's up." I said and then I sat down in the booth. He sat down and gave me direct eye contact.

He said, "You look beautiful."

I can't lie. I stopped home first to change clothes and put myself together. There was no way that I was showing up to see my ex-lover looking all tired and crazy. I showed up to show out, and to let him see what he'd been missing.

I said, "Thank you."

"You look good. I see you healed up." I said.

"Thank you. Yea I did." he responded.

"That is good. When did you cut your hair?" I asked.

He rubbed his head and said, "Um, a while ago." He put his hand back on the table and asked, how have you been?"

"Fine. You?"

"I've been doing great. Um, would you like some coffee?"

"Sure." I said. I watched him get up and go to the counter to order us some coffee. I inhaled and exhaled a few times to get my mind together, but my kitty was still talking. He came back with two cups of coffee, cream, and sugar. He set everything on the table and sat back down.

"I am so happy to finally see you Rae."

I smiled, but I stayed silent as I stirred cream and sugar into my coffee. He took a sip of his coffee and put the cup back on the table.

"Aight. I really wanted to see you, so that I could apologize to you for what went down at your place. I never meant for any of that to happen."

"You've already apologized for that."

"I know, but I know that it was all my fault for not being one hundred percent truthful to either one of you. My plan was to leave my wife for you. I was in the process of making that happen. That was the real reason why I was going to New York. I was looking for places to rent out there, and I was going to ask you to move with me. Yes, I was still having sex with her, and I shouldn't have been. I guess I was being a man."

"I guess so."

"I couldn't figure out a way to leave her without hurting her. I had lost interest in her, and I had fallen in love with you, and I couldn't deny my feelings. I realized either way it went, she was going to get hurt, so I started considering making a move to New York. I miss you so much Rae. I just want to be back in your life."

"So, you can lie to me again?"

"No, so we can be together."

"What happens when you lose interest in me?"

He touched my hand and said, "I'm not. You are everything that I want and need. I don't want anyone else but you."

I felt butterflies when I felt his touch. I pulled my hand away from him to get it together. I broke eye contact and looked down at the table. I couldn't stare into his tantalizing eyes anymore, or I was going to break.

"Raelyn. You can't look at me?" he asked.

I kept my eyes on the napkin on the table.

"Rae?'

"Yes?"

"Look at me."

I looked at him. I was for sure failing the test.

"Did you hear me? I miss you baby." he said. I decided it was time to get out of there. Things were getting deep. I was sticking with the plan. Listen to him and then get out of there before things got deep.

"Um, thanks for the coffee, but I've got to go."

I picked up my purse and slid out of the booth. Before I could stand up, Laron touched my hand again. I felt butterflies again. I looked in his eyes, and then at his lips, and then at his new faded haircut.

"Where are you going?"

"Home."

"Um, can I come by so we can talk some more?"

I paused. I felt my heart about to beat out of my chest.

"Please?" he begged.

I took a deep breath and said, "Ok."

Test failed.

Chapter 17

Raelyn

Not even a minute after we stepped inside my apartment, our lips were locked. He had me up against the wall by my door giving me a passionate kiss. I dropped my purse on the floor next to me, and wrapped my arms around his neck. Laron started rubbing his fingers through my pressed-out hair. He took his lips off mine only to kiss my chin, my neck, and my collar bone, and then he kissed back up my neck to my chin, and then to my lips. When he put his lips back onto mine, I felt his hand on my breasts, and then he slid his hand downwards and under my dress. He started gently rubbing my pearl. I was embarrassed at how wet I was for him. I was too wet, and my kitty was telling the truth about how I had really been feeling. He dipped his finger inside my slippery center. When he felt my waterfall, he moaned, "Ummm."

At that moment, I didn't care what he did to me. I wanted him bad, so I started unbuttoning his jeans. He unzipped my dress. I pulled his shirt off. He pulled my panties down, and then he took off his boxers. I removed my bra while he slid a condom onto his manhood. He picked me up, put himself inside me, and began giving me the business up against the wall. I wrapped my legs and arms around him and took all his inches. We continued to kiss as I lightly dug my nails into his back. There wasn't a lot of moaning between us, but we were into it.

Laron whispered, "Fuck, I missed you."

Hearing that sent me straight to my peak. "I missed you too." I moaned as he continued to rock my ocean up against the wall. He was in it and not stopping. I felt his lips on my neck and then my O hit me. "Ahhh." I moaned out. He felt my walls clinch and he grunted, "Uhhh." Both of us released at the same time, and then we continued to grind into each other and kiss until we both came down from our orgasmic highs. We looked each other in the eyes as I unwrapped my legs from around his waist and put my feet on the floor. He stepped back from me. There was an awkward silence, and then I said, "Um. the bathroom is around the corner and the towels are in the closet."

He said, "Thanks. I like your new place by the way."

"Thanks." I said.

He picked his clothes up from the floor and walked into my bathroom. As soon as I heard the bathroom door close, I started cussing myself out.

I whispered, "Damn Raelyn! What the hell is your problem? Why did you do that? That was stupid!" I started pacing back and forth while rubbing my fingers through my hair. I heard him turn the sink off, so I hurriedly picked my clothes up off the floor and changed my demeanor to look like I wasn't tripping. Laron walked out of the bathroom as I was throwing my clothes into my hamper. He was fully dressed. I slid into my terry cloth robe. There was some more awkward silence between us.

He said, "Um. I can leave if you want."

I said, "You don't have to."

He said, "I didn't plan for this to happen. I really just wanted to talk."

"It's not your fault. It takes two."

We paused again. There were a few seconds of more awkward silence and then I asked, "Are you hungry?"

He smiled, walked over to me, and gave me a hug.

"I was thinking that you were going to put me out." he said.

"Trust me, I thought about it, but I'm not." I smiled, and then I said. "Let me get cleaned up and then I can hook us up something."

***

I woke up lying next to Laron in my bed. It was early evening, but the sun was still shining bright in the sky. I looked at my phone to see what time it was. I saw a missed call from my sister from a couple of hours earlier. I had been sleep all day with Laron. I hadn't slept that good in a while. It was crazy how having him next to me could change how I slept. He had me wrapped up in his arms and I was snuggled tight against his body. The feeling of his body heat next to mine made me feel safe and warm. We hadn't laid next to each other in my bed since the night that the shooting incident happened in my bedroom. The thought of the shooting went through my mind and made me feel a little anxiety, so I lightly removed his arm from around my body and slid out of bed. I tip-toed to my front door to make sure that the door was locked and the chain was on. After I checked the door, I turned around and started looking around my place to make sure no one was in there. I didn't know if he was lying about being divorced, but I did not need Paris to come lurking for her husband again. I checked behind my curtains, in my closets, behind the shower curtain in my bathroom, and under my bed. Hell, I even checked the cabinets. Chicks will do anything in the name of love. I didn't see anything, so I walked back into the room. The bed moved when I laid back down next to Laron and it woke him up.

He rubbed his eyes and asked, "What's wrong?"

"Nothing."

"What time is it?"

"A little after six o'clock."

"Damn we've been sleeping that long?"

"Yea."

He pulled me to him and kissed my shoulder, my neck, and then my cheek.

He said, "I missed you so much baby. I'm glad that we are back together."

"Just because we had sex doesn't mean we are back together."

"Ok you got that, but it could mean that we are working on it."

"I guess you can say that." I said, and from that day forward, me and Laron were back at it again.

Chapter 18

Aleyah

"Baby, when will Niko and Faye be here?" Aleyah asked Lamar as she flipped the chicken frying in the pan.

"Soon." Lamar said when he walked into their kitchen.

Aleyah said, "Ok." She turned the stove off and began putting the fried chicken onto a paper towel covered plate. Lamar walked up to her and hugged her from behind.

"You look and smell damn good baby."

"Thank you." Aleyah said. She finished putting the chicken onto the plate.

Aleyah had been thinking about and fantasizing about Niko since they went to the red-light party. She decided that she would mention making an invitation to Niko for a little bedroom fun. The last couple of times she had sex with her husband only lasted ten minutes tops, and she was bored. He gave her some good head, but Aleyah was ready for some sexual excitement.

"What do you think about Niko and Faye? You know, and us?"

"My best friend, baby?"

"Yea. What? We did my best friend."

"I know and we've done other couples, but never Niko."

"So, we can do my friend, but we can't do yours?"

"That's not what I am saying. I'm just surprised that you like him like that."

"I like him and Faye. I think they are cool, sexy, and fun like us. Plus, I know that you like Faye. I can tell how you look at her. I've seen you looking at her booty a time or two. Hell, I looked at that thing too."

Lamar laughed, "I guess I've checked her out."

"We haven't done it in a while, and I am ready for some fun, so what do you think?"

"You know that I'm down for whatever your down for baby. We know the rules."

"Yup. What we do in the bedroom stays in the bedroom. Never step outside of us."

"Yup."

"Do you think that he will be down?"

"Hell yea. Niko has always been into freaky shit. He'll probably be flattered."

Aleyah laughed and took her apron off. "Well you know how we work it."

"Yup."

After swinging a few times in Atlanta, Aleyah brought her best friend Karina in the bedroom once when she was in town for a visit. Karina was down for the experience because she had just broken up with her baby's father. Aleyah hoped the experience with Niko would be just as fun. After Aleyah saw Niko giving it to Faye at the party, she knew that she wanted him, but only if it she could talk her husband into it. She cleaned up the stove, and then she heard the doorbell. Aleyah and Lamar walked to the door to answer it.

"Sup bruh." Niko said when they opened the door.

"Sup bruh" Lamar replied before slapping hands with Niko.

The ladies hugged. "Hey lady." Faye said to Aleyah.

"You guys come in and have a seat, we are going to eat out here in the living room."

"Aight. Do you mind if I roll this up?" Niko asked. He pulled a bag of marijuana out of his jeans pocket.

"Go ahead bruh." Lamar said.

Faye and Niko sat down on the couch. Niko pulled a Swisher Sweet cigar out of his pocket, licked it down the middle, and then used his thumb nails to split the cigar. Aleyah was happy that Niko brought something to smoke with him. She knew that it would be a good night of making love for her and Lamar. Sometimes she wished that he would get high every day, so he could put it on her like the porn stars in the freaky movies she watches. Getting high and group sex seems to be the only way to bring the freak out of him the way she likes it.

"What y'all drinking tonight? We got wine, Cîroc, Hennessey, and Crown Royal Apple." Lamar said.

Faye and Niko said, "Crown."

"Aight, I got y'all."

Lamar went to fix their drinks, while Aleyah made their plates. Aleyah was in her element again. Cooking and hosting for her friends. She loved having company over even if there was no agenda. Aleyah gave Niko and Faye their plates and Lamar gave them their drinks. They sat down with them to eat. They had music on and a movie playing on the television, but they were doing more talking. After everyone ate, they got a game of spades going. They decided to do girls against guys. Niko lit up the blunt and passed it around. Aleyah happily accepted it, took several hits, and then passed it to her husband. Lamar hit it and reached to pass it to Faye.

"Hold up bae. That was a baby hit." Aleyah said through chuckles. She was laughing, but she was serious. She wanted to make sure he was feeling stimulated. Faye and Niko laughed as Lamar hit the blunt a few more times.

He passed it to Faye and said, "You see how she is? A little drill Sargent."

Everyone laughed and then Aleyah said, "Be quiet bae. No, I am not."

"You're shitting me. You know that you are the boss in this house. She runs everything inside and outside of this house, my life, her life, and our son's life."

Aleyah laughed and said, "I ain't bossy. I consider myself a manager. I keep things organized."

Faye said, "I feel you on that girl."

"Ah hell nah. You ain't about to try to do me like that." Niko said through laughs.

"Don't let her bruh. She will take over." Lamar said.

"Not going to happen." Niko said.

"Anyways. That's game. We win again." Faye said. She slapped hands with Aleyah, and the guys shook their heads.

After about an hour of playing, Niko rolled up another blunt, and Aleyah refilled everyone's glasses. They were all feeling buzzed and high, and the ladies were whooping the guys in spades.

"You two are trying to beat us up really bad." Lamar said. They ladies laughed and gave each other a high five.

"That shit ain't right y'all." Niko said.

"Oh, be quiet, stop whining." Faye said and then she began laughing with Aleyah. Lamar frowned, and then Aleyah said. "Aww baby. I'm sorry. Give me a kiss." She leaned over and gave her husband a passionate kiss with tongue. She felt Niko's eyes on them.

Niko took a pull from the blunt, and then he asked, "Y'all tryna hit The Red Light again this weekend?" He passed it to Aleyah.

Aleyah took the blunt and said, "Yup, if we don't have little man. Are you down baby?" She took a few pulls from the blunt and then passed it to Lamar. He took the blunt from her and answered, "Yea." The way Lamar was leaned back in his chair she could tell that he was feeling good. She was instantly turned on. She decided it would be the best time to push the conversation in the direction that she wanted it to go.

Aleyah took the blunt back from Lamar, took a pull from it, and said, "The red-light party was fun." she passed the blunt to Faye.

Niko said, "Hell yea. It was the shit. I was fucked up that night."

"We were too." Aleyah said.

Lamar said, "I didn't even know they threw parties like that in Minnesota."

"Hell yea. All the time." Faye said.

"We used to go to them in Atlanta all the time. A friend of mine invited me the first time." Aleyah said.

Faye said, "We go all the time."

Niko said, "We get invites by email, or through a private group on our social media pages. I can have my boy add you to the email list and the group, if you want."

"Yea you can. I didn't even know you got down like that Niko." Aleyah said.

Faye laughed, "Oh, well then you don't know Niko."

Niko laughed. "I do a little something, something when I am in the mood."

Have y'all ever done something with another couple before?" Aleyah asked.

"I have once." Niko said.

"I've never done it, but I'm open to whatever. I am what you call a try-sexual because I'll try anything at least once." Faye said and then joined in loud laughter.

"Anything?" Lamar asked.

"Almost, but I ain't down with urine, feces, doing animals. It ain't that deep."

"Ewww." Lamar said.

"I'm just saying. There are some people that are into some weird fetish type shit."

"True, but I ain't with it either." Aleyah laughed.

"What about y'all? Have you done other couples?" Niko asked.

"Yup, many times." Aleyah said.

"What bruh?" Niko asked. He had shocked look on his face.

"Yea. I thought you knew that?"

"Nah you ain't never told me that. I knew y'all liked freaky shit, but I didn't know that y'all got down like that." Niko said.

Aleyah decided to throw it out there. "Yea we do. Would y'all be down to join us?" she asked.

"For real bruh?" Niko said.

"Yea. Only if you with it." Lamar said.

"Hell, yea I'm with it." Niko said with a smile.

Faye said, "Y'all know I'm down for whatever. I was watching y'all at the red-light like damn." Everyone laughed, and then Niko asked, "How far though bruh? We swapping?" Niko said.

"Yea, if Faye is cool with that."

"I'm down."

Aleyah smiled. It worked out just the way she wanted it.

***

A couple drinks later they were all intertwined in Lamar and Aleyah's bed. The ladies wasted no time swapping. Aleyah crawled over to Niko and took him into her mouth Faye did the same to Lamar. Niko was standing there with his chocolate bar in hand; watching his flesh disappear between Aleyah's lips. Aleyah devoured him hungrily. She was extremely turned on by him and excited to get a taste of him.

"Ah yea. That's right." Niko said. Aleyah responded with moans and slurps as she bobbed her head up and down on Niko. She could hear Faye going to work on Lamar next to them. She heard Lamar say, "Damn girl." Aleyah looked at them out of the corner of her eye. Faye was deep throating her husband. He was in a zone with his eyes closed. Niko hadn't taken his eyes off Aleyah.

"Look up at me beautiful." he said. Aleyah gave Niko the eye contact that he asked for.

"You like that?" she asked.

"Um hum." Niko responded.

"Damn bruh, wifey is the truth." he said to Lamar.

"Shorty got that work too bruh." Lamar responded. They slapped hands.

Niko turned his attention back to Aleyah. "I like that shit." he said.

Aleyah heard her husband groan. He stepped back from Faye and said, "Damn girl." She knew that meant that he was trying to get control so he wouldn't bust too fast.

"I want to see the ladies go at it." Niko said.

"I do too." Lamar responded.

Aleyah smiled, backed up from Niko, and crawled over to Faye. She kissed Faye passionately, and then pushed her backwards so she would lay down. Aleyah put her tongue on Faye's pearl and flicked it a few times before sucking it. They guys stood back and watched the show for a while, and then Lamar walked over to Faye and put his manhood back into her mouth. Niko made his way over to Aleyah. Niko smacked Aleyah's butt.

"Let me see what that pussy feels like." he said. Aleyah got up on her knees without taking her mouth off Faye. Niko entered her from behind.

"Mmmm." Aleyah moaned when she felt Niko inside of her. He felt exactly how she'd fantasized. Niko squeezed her butt as he pounded into her with slow, aggressive thrusts. Aleyah bounced back as she continued to give Faye oral. Faye was lying on her back; giving Lamar oral. Aleyah felt Niko hit her spot, so she moaned louder. Lamar pulled his manhood out of Faye's mouth to gain control again. He stepped back and watched the other three go at it for a few minutes, and then he told Faye to come to him. Faye crawled over to Lamar and bent over doggy style for him. Aleyah heard Faye moaning as her Lamar put his pound game on her. When he was in his zone, his pound game was on point. Niko pulled out of Aleyah and told her to get on top of him. He laid on his back and then Aleyah climbed on top of him. Lamar pulled out of Faye to catch himself again.

"Damn girl you're going to make me cum." Lamar said. Niko chuckled and then he smacked Aleyah on the ass. Faye crawled over to Niko and put her blossom on his face. The two women worked on Niko until Lamar rejoined the party.

"You want double baby?"

"Yea." Aleyah moaned.

Lamar walked over to her and put his manhood into Aleyah's backside. Aleyah moaned when she felt the two men inside of her. She was in her zone; feeling pleasure on another level.

"Ahhhh." she moaned.

"You like that baby?" Lamar asked.

"Yes. Don't stop." she moaned as she watched Niko giving Faye oral.

"You gonna cum?"

"Yes." Aleyah cried out as she felt the two men inside of her. She heard Niko moan when he felt her walls tighten. Faye cried out from an orgasm and collapsed on the side of them. Niko and Lamar continued to work on Aleyah until she cried out that she was having an orgasm. Lamar pulled out and let himself go right after her, and then Niko told her to lift when he got his. The four of them lay on various parts of the King size bed trying to catch their breath, and then Niko said, "That shit was the truth."

"You damn right." Lamar chuckled. Aleyah crawled over to her husband and kissed him.

"Thank you, baby." she whispered, and then she said, "Y'all hungry?"

"Hell yea." Niko chuckled.

"Cool, I'm about to hook us up some breakfast."

Nia Rich

Chapter 19

Riley

"I am going to kill that bitch!" Riley yelled into the phone.

"What? What happened?" Raelyn asked as she was folding her laundry on her bed. She folded a shirt and then she sat down on the bed to give her sister her undivided attention. She had never heard her sister that angry, so she knew that it wasn't good.

"She put a brick through my car window, spray painted the word bitch down the side of my car, and popped all my tires!"

Raelyn's eyebrows went up and her eyes opened wide. "No way." she said.

"Yes sister! I am standing outside of my house looking at it now!"

"I'm on my way." Raelyn hung up the phone.

Riley wiped a tear and then called Jamir. When Jamir answered the phone, she said, "That crazy bitch destroyed my car! I am going to kill her!" she wiped some more tears.

"Huh? Slow down bae. What happened?" he asked.

"There is a brick in my window, and bitch sprayed all down the side! This is going to cost a fortune to fix! I don't have that kind of money! When I see that bitch, I am fucking her up!"

"Don't talk like that. I am on my way." Jamir hung up the phone.

Riley leaned her back up against her car and put one of her hands on her forehead. She felt like her head was going to explode. She wanted to jump in the car with the window broken and the spray paint down the side to go and find that girl. She looked down at the ground and let the sun burn her back. She shook her head side to side and then she heard a car pull up. Riley looked up and saw that it was her sister. Raelyn parked in front of Riley's car and got out wearing a baseball cap with her hair in a ponytail. She pulled her fitted baseball cap down over her eyes to block the sun.

"Damn sister." she said when she approached Riley.

Riley looked up and said, "Do you see this shit!?" pointing at the car.

Raelyn walked around the car to get a good look at the damage. The word, 'Bitch,' was sprayed painted in bright red letters down the driver's side of the car. The brick was thrown through the driver's side window, but it looked like someone tried to throw it through the windshield first. Raelyn shook her head and walked over to her sister. She wrapped her arms around Riley and hugged her.

"I'm sorry sister." Raelyn said.

Riley wiped some tears and said, "Thanks."

Raelyn hugged her sister in silence for a moment, and then she asked, "Have you learned your lesson yet?"

"Sister don't start." Riley said as she pushed Raelyn away. She dried her tears with the back of her hand and turned to look back at the car.

"Don't start what? Telling the truth?" Raelyn asked.

"Not right now." Riley said.

"Alright, well, don't you have a restraining order on her. Call the police and file a report, and then call your insurance company."

"You're right. I am going to do that. Put her dumb ass in jail for a while."

Riley swiped the screen on her cell phone to unlock it. She started dialing the emergency number when Jamir pulled up. She stopped dialing the number and turned her attention to Jamir. Jamir jumped out of his car and walked straight to Riley.

"Bae, I am sorry." he said while hugging her. "Hey Rae." he said to Raelyn before kissing Riley on the lips. Raelyn stepped back with a frown on her face. She folded her arms. She didn't speak back. She wanted to smack the shit out of Jamir.

"Jamir, I am calling the police on that bitch." Riley said.

"No bae. Wait." he said.

"What do you mean wait? Look at my car!" Riley yelled.

Jamir spoke softly to her. "I know. I know, but I can't have the mother of my child in jail. I am going to take care of everything. I got you. It will be fixed up and brand new immediately. I will pay for everything. Don't worry."

"Jamir."

"I know bae. I got you. She ain't going to mess with you anymore, alright?" He kissed Riley on the forehead. Riley calmed down immediately. Raelyn was disgusted at how her sister turned to mush for Jamir. She shook her head, and then saw a guy pull up and get out of his car. Raelyn noticed how attractive he was. He was wearing a pair of jean shorts with a polo style shirt, a pair of all white Nikes, and he had sunglasses on his face. He was carrying a bag full of books from a book store. He looked a bit older than the three of them, but he was well put together.

"Is everything alright out here." he asked as he looked at the car.

"Yea bruh. We good." Jamir said to him.

"Aight." he said. Raelyn watched the man walk up the stairs to the porch and into the downstairs apartment.

Damn he was fine, she thought. She turned her attention back to Riley and Jamir.

"I am going to have my uncle come now to pick up your car and tow it to my boys detailing shop, and then we will go and get you a rental."

"Ok." Riley said. Jamir stepped away with his phone to his ear.

Raelyn rolled her eyes. "I'm leaving sister. Call me if you need me." she said. They hugged and then Raelyn got into her car and pulled off.

*** .

"I love you, bae." Riley moaned.

"I know you do." Jamir told Riley as he pounded into her.

He pulled out and put his mouth on her peach. Riley cried out a few obscenities as he licked her into an orgasm. While her body shivered, he put his manhood back into her. He pounded into her until she stopped shivering and then he flipped her over on her stomach. Riley grabbed a handful of sheets and bit into a pillow as Jamir gave her his thug stroke.

"Yes. Go deeper bae." Riley moaned.

"That's that spot ain't it?"

"Yeaaaa baeeeee." she whined before he smacked her backside as hard as he could. He pounded more aggressively. She took every thrust like a professional.

"Take this d girl." he said, and then he smacked her backside again extremely hard.

"Yes daddy. I love you." she moaned.

"Who's daddy?"

"Youuuuu." Riley moaned. He pushed her hips flat to the bed, leaned forward and whispered in her ear, "You wanna have my baby?"

"Yes. I wanna have your baby."

"You gonna cum for daddy?"

"Yeeeessss. I'm cuming." Riley screeched into the pillow.

"That's right. You gonna have my baby."

"Yes daddy. I will." she moaned. Jamir continued to pound into Riley until he spilled his liquid into Riley. He pulled out of her and kissed her on the shoulder. She turned over onto her back, wrapped her arms around his neck, and said, "I love you."

Chapter 20

Raelyn

I sent a response text to Shawn telling him that I was having a good night and confirming that I would visit his job the next day. I put my phone down and turned my attention back to Laron who was finishing up a phone call. We were sitting in the fifth-floor parking lot of the Mall of America. I was waiting for Laron to finish his phone call so we could go inside to the movie theaters. Sitting out there made me think about the last time we went out. I was with him and Paris. It was one of the last times we all hung out before we split and I became the side chick. An image of Paris holding the gun in the dark crossed my mind, and then thoughts of my sister took over.

"Are you ready?" Laron asked after he finished his call.

"Yup." I said. I pulled the visor mirror down to apply some more lip gloss, and then I said, "I have a question."

"What's up?" Laron asked.

I put the visor mirror back up. "Is your boy Jamir still married?"

"Honestly, I don't know. Me and Jamir are cool, but we aren't that close. Why?"

"I don't know. My sister is just going through some stuff with him, and I don't want her to end up in a situation like ours."

"Yea. I understand."

"Speaking of that, I never asked you. What happened to Paris? Is she locked up?"

"Nah, she isn't. I never pressed charges. We divorced and then she moved back to Cali."

"Oh."

"Yea. That situation is behind me now. I hope that it's behind you too. I am trying to start fresh with you now that I have you back."

"It is." I lied. Part of me was, but part of me still wasn't sure if I could trust him. I still worried that Paris may show up again with her gun to pop me. I opened the car and got out of the car. Laron took my hand into his and we walked into the mall.

***

"Your new place is nice." I said as I walked through Laron's new apartment. It was clean and well organized. There was no sign of a woman being there anywhere in the place.

"Yea I decided to downsize after the divorce. There was no point in me living in a big house by myself." Laron said. I looked around the place and nodded my head. Laron looked at me and asked, "What's wrong baby?"

"Nothing."

He walked over to me, hugged me, and said, "It's just me here. I promise. There is no need to feel uncomfortable."

I smiled and nodded my head. I was tripping a little bit. It was my first time at his new place.

"I know. I like it for real." I said.

"Good. Sit down and make yourself comfortable."

I sat down on the couch and Laron disappeared towards the back of the apartment. I heard water running, and then he came back into the living room, and said, "Come here." I stood up and followed him to the back of the apartment where the bathroom was. He had candles lit around a bathtub full of bubbles.

"Get undressed and get in. I'll be right back."

I smiled. That was the romantic and thoughtful stuff I loved about him. I got undressed and slid down into the steamy bubble bath. Laron came back with bath towels, a bottle of champagne, and a glass. He poured champagne into the glass and handed it to me and then he rolled the sleeves of his shirt up. He dipped one of the bath towels into the warm water and squeezed warm water onto my back. I took a sip and then I enjoyed the feeling of Laron washing my body. After he finished washing my body he helped me step out of the bathtub. He dried my body off and then he told me that he would meet me in the bedroom.

After he gave me a full body massage, he took a shower and met me in the bedroom. He slid under the covers, kissed me and then climbed on top of me. I wrapped my legs around him and let him enter me. He did everything slow. He kissed me slow, he grinded into me slow, he switched positions slow. He whispered that he loved me repeatedly. I repeated the same to him, I moaned his name, I rode his stroke, I sucked on his neck, I told him where to put it, and not to stop. We made that headboard make rhythmic drum sounds up against the wall. I sang orgasmic melodies over the drum sounds from the headboard, and then I released my rainfall onto him. He busted while I reached my peak, and then I passed out in his arms.

Chapter 21

Raelyn

As I sat behind the desk at the community center, I watched how Shawn interacted with the kids. Every kid that walked through the door was happy to see him. They showed him a lot of love and respect. The community center had kids of all ages.

"Who is this Mr. Shawn." one of the teenage boys asked.

"That is his girlfriend." one of the girls said.

Shawn said, "She is my friend you guys. Her name is Ms. Raelyn. Say hi."

"Hi Ms. Raelyn." the kids said.

"Hi." I said and smiled.

One of the girls said, "You are pretty."

"Thank you, I responded. All the kids were crowding around the desk staring at me. I felt like an ornament on a tree, or a new puppy home from the pet store.

"Alright you guys. Go and busy yourself. No fighting in the gym. You hear me?"

"Yes Mr. Shawn." they responded, and then they dispersed to separate parts of the community center. Shawn sat down in the chair next to me.

"They seem to really like you." I said.

"Yea they do. I love these kids like they are mine."

"So you don't have children?"

"No. No yet."

"Wow."

"Yea. I thought me and my ex would of, but it never happened. I am kind of glad though because I wasn't looking for a baby mama anyways. I want a wife and a family. Something I didn't grow up with."

"I understand."

"What about you? Do you want kids?" Shawn asked.

"Well, yea, one day. I was raised in a two parent, Christian home, so it's an expectation in my family to be married before kids. I don't want to be baby mama."

"That's good."

"I don't want to disappoint my parents; unlike my brother who has already done that by not marrying his baby mama. They were extremely angry with him. I don't want to face their wrath."

Shawn chuckled. "You are so beautiful to me." He touched my chin. I blushed. "Thank you."

"You're going to make a good man happy one day." he said. I smiled. One of the kids walked up to the desk and asked him to come to the arts and crafts room. I followed him to the room and watched him in his element. With all the negativity in the news about our black men and our youth, it was nice to see them doing positive things. It made me more attracted to Shawn.

As we walked back to the desk, he asked, "Are you busy Sunday?"

"No."

"Would you like to go to church with me?"

"Church?"

He laughed. "Yes, Church."

"You go to church?"

"Yes. I go to church every Sunday. My mom would kill me if I didn't show up. You tryna go?"

"Um. Yea. Sure."

"Aight cool. I will text you the info."

Chapter 22

Aleyah

Aleyah was lying on the couch with her husband watching television. They were having a quiet night at home without their son. Aleyah was watching television, but her mind was other places. She was in the mood for some back breaking sex. With little man gone, it was the perfect time to have some wild and crazy sex, do it all over the house, and make as much noise as they wanted to. She knew Lamar wasn't going to last long enough to give her that kind of pleasure. She rolled her eyes and thought about getting him drunk and high, so she could get a little more than the usual out of him.

"It feels good not to have little man again." Aleyah said.

"Yea. He is never home these days." Lamar said.

"I know. Since we moved home, everyone wants him to come over. He has more of a social life then us." Aleyah said.

"I know. Between play dates, birthday parties, and your mom, we've had a babysitter almost every weekend." Lamar said.

"I ain't complaining." Aleyah said.

"Me either." Lamar said.

There was a moment of silence and then Aleyah said, "We should go out tonight babe."

"Nah baby. I just wanted to enjoy a relaxing night at home with my wife." Lamar said.

"Well, let's get high." Aleyah said.

Lamar made a screw face and said, "What makes you want to do that? You know we only do that every now and then."

"I know babe, but I want to have some fun."

"Babe, spending time with you is fun."

"Yea, but we don't have little man, so we should let loose."

"Look. I ain't tryna do a bunch of stuff. If you want to get high, go ahead."

"I don't know where to get it." Aleyah said.

"You know Niko has everything. Call him. I am sure he wouldn't mind bringing it by."

Aleyah felt frustrated. Her plan was not working. There was no point in her getting high by herself. She needed him to get stimulated too, so he could do her the way she wanted.

"Alright. You call him."

Lamar made the call and Niko showed up about thirty minutes later. Aleyah felt instant attraction when she saw Niko. She felt her box get wet, when he kissed her on the cheek, and said, "Hey beautiful."

"Hey Niko." she said. Her mind went straight to the night they had the foursome. She saw an image of herself on top of him and then she shook the thought. Niko walked in and greeted Lamar. "Sup bruh." he said after slapping hands with him.

"Ain't shit bruh. Wifey got me trying to get something." Lamar said.

"Ah you tryna get high Aleyah?"

Aleyah laughed and said, "Yea. I'm tryna get us high, but he ain't with it, so I guess that it's just me tonight."

"I hear that. Well, here y'all go. It's on me. Don't worry about it." Niko handed Lamar a bag of weed.

"Nah bruh. Let me pay you."

"Nah. I'm good. Y'all enjoy your night."

"Aight thanks bruh."

"No problem. Y'all need a blunt?"

"Yea." Aleyah said.

Niko handed a swisher sweet to Aleyah. When she caught eye contact with him, she felt her mouth salivate a little. His nails were clean, his muscles were bulging out of his t-shirt, his tattoos were oiled up and noticeable, his haircut was fresh. She wanted him.

Aleyah said, "Thank you."

"Aight fam, I'm out. I got to go pick Faye up. We are about to go out."

Aleyah felt jealous when he said that. She wished her and Lamar were going out. "Oh ok. Well, have fun and tell her that I said hi."

"I will." Niko said as he walked to the door. Aleyah followed him to the door, closed and locked it after he left. She walked back to the living room and sat on the couch.

"See they are going out."

"So, that is them."

Aleyah rolled her eyes and started breaking down the weed. She rolled the blunt up and lit it. She took a couple of puffs and said, "Here hit this."

'Nah babe. I told you I was good."

"Come on babe. Just a little. Please." she begged.

"Aight. Damn Aleyah you on some other shit tonight." He took the blunt and took a few small hits and then he gave it back to her. Aleyah knew that it wasn't enough to make him give her that jungle loving, but she would take what she could get. She smoked half the blunt alone and then she laid back down and put her hands on his manhood. Lamar laid there until he felt his manhood getting hard.

"I want you." Aleyah said.

Lamar took his eyes off the television and kissed Aleyah. He didn't say a word he just pulled his manhood out and climbed on top of her. He pulled her pajama pants and panties off and put his manhood inside of her. Lamar kept his eyes on her as he began pumping in and out of her. He kissed her again and then she closed her eyes. She began fantasizing about Niko. She didn't do it purposely, but thoughts of him popped into her head. She started moaning loudly as her husband pumped in and out of her, and before she knew it, she was getting hers.

"Ahhh." she cried out when her orgasm hit her, and then it was over. Lamar lost himself and busted right after her. He rested his head on her shoulder as he let himself go. *Uuugh.* she thought to herself. Lamar kissed her, got up, and walked to the bathroom to clean up. Aleyah rolled her eyes and sat up. She couldn't wait for him to go to sleep, so she could watch some porn and pleasure herself.

***

Aleyah slammed down her drink fast and asked for a refill.

"Dang girl. Slow down." Raelyn said.

"Yea your drinking too fast. I haven't even finished my first one." Riley said.

"I am just happy to be out of the house." Aleyah said.

"You're acting like you never get out." Raelyn said.

"Not enough. I'm tired of sitting at home." Aleyah said.

"Don't you and Lamar go out?" Riley asked.

"We did sometimes when we were living in Atlanta, but since we moved home, it's like he hasn't wanted to go out at all. He wants to sit home and watch T.V. and movies like an old married couple."

"There is nothing wrong with being at home with your man." Riley said.

"I know, but every night? I want to have some fun." Aleyah said.

Raelyn looked at Riley and then she said, "Sounds like it's more than that." Raelyn said.

Aleyah took another gulp of her drink and said, "I'm not going to lie y'all. I'm bored in my marriage."

"Bored like how?" Raelyn asked.

"He is boring. Sex is boring. I am bored overall. I have been for years."

"Wow." Riley said.

"Have you told him?" Raelyn asked.

"How do you tell your man that you are bored with him?" Aleyah asked.

"Just keep it one hundred. It's not what you say. It's how you say it." Raelyn said.

"I don't know. We love each other, and we have good times, but I am not genuinely happy. Sometimes it feels like he isn't that into me anymore either. I think we are growing apart."

"Talk to him. I'm sure it's fixable." Riley said.

"Yea. You're right. So, what's up with you two?" Riley are you still messing with that dude?"

A smile spread across Riley's face. "Yes. That's my bae." she said.

Raelyn rolled her eyes and said, "Tell her what happened to your car." Aleyah looked at Riley and asked, "What happened?"

"His ex bitch wrecked it."

"Shut up." Aleyah said.

"Yea girl. Threw a brick through the window. Spray paint and all." Raelyn said.

"Yea, but my bae fixed it and it's all brand new again. Looks better than it did before she wrecked it. I thanked him over and over again." Riley said with a smile.

Aleyah said, "Girl, that chick is crazy." Aleyah said.

"Yea, *for her* man." Raelyn said.

"Please. He don't love that hoe. He loves me, so she can trip all she wants. We are still going to be together." Riley said.

Raelyn shook her head. "Anyways, it's going to be a fun time tonight celebrating Eazy's birthday and Riley's last day at the club." Raelyn said.

"Aww congrats on your new job Ri!" Aleyah said.

"Thank sis." Riley said. Aleyah noticed how much she was glowing; she looked happy. The same way Aleyah used to look when she first got with Lamar.

"I know. I am proud of you and mad at you at the same time. I don't even want to think about it because I'll start crying again."

"I'm going to miss you sister." Riley said. She reached out to hug her sister. Raelyn hugged her back and said, "I know. I'm going to miss you more. Ok. Don't start. I don't want to mess up my make up." The doorbell rang so Raelyn and Riley released their embrace and walked to the door to let Cherry and Taji in.

"It's party time bitches!" Taji said.

"Hey ladies!" Raelyn said.

"Now that we all are here. Let's take a shot for Riley." Aleyah said.

"Alright now, don't get wasted Aleyah because I'm not in the business for babysitting."

"I'm good y'all." Aleyah said.

"Alright." Raelyn sang as she poured Patron into five shot glasses.

They held up their glasses, and then Raelyn said, "To Ri's new job." They clinked glasses together and took the shot. After everyone swallowed their shots, Cherry said, "No fighting tonight twins. You too Taji."

The three of them replied, "We good."

Chapter 23

Aleyah

Aleyah and the ladies spent most of the night in Eazy's VIP section drinking and partying with him and his friends. Aleyah was glad they stayed behind the rope because she was so tipsy that if a fight popped off, she wouldn't have been able to defend herself, or help anyone else.

They had just finished dancing to a Cardi B song when Taji announced that she was leaving. She said that she needed to get home for a photoshoot in the morning. After the ladies hugged her goodbye, Aleyah told the girls that she needed to sit down because her feet were hurting. She walked over to one of the velvet couches and sat down. She took a video clip of herself at the club and then she posted it to her social media page. She put her phone back into her purse and then began watching everyone in the VIP section doing their thing. Her eyes rested on Eazy. He always had a swag and confidence about himself. It was present in the way he walked, talked, and dressed. She looked over his outfit for the night. He was 2Pac the night at the MGM Grand fresh. He was wearing a dress shirt with dress pants, gold chain, watch, nice shoes. He always looked good to her, but she would never admit it to him or anyone else. Aleyah and Eazy had crushes on each other growing up, but they were raised to look at each other as siblings, so they never acted on their feelings for each other. Aleyah often wondered what life would've been like if she would have married Eazy instead of Lamar. Aleyah saw Eazy look her way, so she turned her attention back to her phone. She got a social media message that said, *I'm out too. Where you at?* It was a message from Niko. She responded and told him what club she was at. He responded, *I'm about to slide through.* She blackout the screen on her phone as Eazy approached her.

"Are you good?" Eazy asked.

"Yes, I am Eazy" Aleyah responded.

She felt butterflies in her stomach. Eazy was her best friend growing up, and he was the first guy that she'd ever loved. She had learned how to suppress her thoughts and feelings, but every time he was around her, they would resurface. She had gotten good at hiding them, even though deep down inside he was the man she really wanted to be with. Aleyah remembered days when she would day dream about running away with Eazy to get married and live happily ever after without anyone finding out. She married her husband Lamar because she accidentally got pregnant and didn't want her parents to know that she was having sex before marriage, and she certainly couldn't have a baby out of wedlock. Eazy and Aleyah had never expressed feelings for each other growing up, but she remembered how disappointed Eazy looked when he found out about the pregnancy and marriage. Aleyah felt the same when she found out that Eazy had gotten his girlfriend pregnant months before.

Aleyah smiled at Eazy as he sat down next to her and asked, "Why are you sitting down? Are your dogs barking?"

"Yea they are." she responded.

He laughed, "That's what you women get trying to be all cute in shoes that aren't comfortable."

"You men like it." she said

"You're right we do. I haven't had the chance to talk to you since you've been home." he said.

"I know." she said.

"How have you been?"

"I've been good. How about you?"

"I've been doing me. You know. We should catch up, if that is cool with you?"

"You know it's cool with me Eazy."

"Cool. Put my number in your phone and call me."

Aleyah pulled her phone out of her purse and saved Eazy's number to it, and then she called his phone. When he got the call, he said, "Alright. I am going to hit you up. You look good by the way." he said as he stood up.

Aleyah smiled and said, "Thanks Eazy."

After Eazy walked away, Aleyah got a text from Niko saying that he was in the club. She looked around the club and spotted him at the bar with a pair of ripped up black jeans and a button up shirt on. She took in how fine he was from a far. She got a flash back of how he felt inside of her the night they had the foursome. She stood up and left the VIP area and headed to where Niko was.

"Hey! she said with a smile when she walked up.

"What's up beautiful?" he said as he gave her a hug.

"Where's Faye?"

"Oh, I dropped her off at the crib. She had something to do in the morning and didn't want to stay out too late. I was in the mood to be out and about, and I saw that you were out, so I decided to slide through. Where's bro?"

"Lamar is at home with little man. I am out with my girls tonight."

"Oh alright. I see. Well, you are looking good tonight."

Aleyah smiled. "Thanks. You too." she said.

"Take a shot with your boy. What you drinking boo?"

"Patron."

"Aight." Niko said. He ordered two shots from the bartender. He handed one to Aleyah. She smiled at him and then they swallowed down their shots. He asked, "You tryna smoke?"

Aleyah said, "Sure."

"Cool. Let's go to my car."

"Alright. Let me tell my girls and I will meet you outside."

The twins and Cherry were watching Aleyah the whole time.

"Who is that dude, she is talking to?" Cherry asked. "He looks familiar." she said.

"I was thinking the same thing when I first met him." Riley said.

"Y'all know him?" Cherry asked.

"That is her husband's friend, if I am not mistaken. He was at the dinner she invited us to." Raelyn said.

"Husband's friend my ass. Anybody with eyes can see they were flirting." Cherry said.

"Yup. That is him. He is fine as hell, but I feel like I've seen him before that." Riley said.

They stopped talking when Aleyah approached them.

"Hey!" she said excitedly. "Are we still going to the pizza spot after this?" she asked.

"Yea." Riley said.

"Who was that?" Cherry asked.

"That is a friend of me and my husbands. I am going outside for a second. I'll meet y'all at the pizza place."

"Ok." Raelyn responded.

Aleyah met Niko outside and followed him to his car. She slid into the passenger side of his Jeep Wrangler. He cracked the windows and sparked up a blunt that was already rolled. He took a few long pulls. Clouds of smoke filled the car as he inhaled and then blew smoke out of his mouth and nose. He handed Aleyah the blunt. After he blew more smoke out of his mouth and nose, he asked, "Were you and your girls out celebrating or were you just out?"

"We were out celebrating their brother's birthday." Aleyah said before blowing smoke out of her nose.

"Aw ok. That's what's up." he said as he took the blunt she passed back. "Real talk, I wouldn't have let you out of my sight, if I was bruh."

Aleyah giggled. "Why?" she asked.

"Not looking like that. You are too fine and your looking too damn good in that dress."

Aleyah giggled again. "Thanks."

I'm just saying." he chuckled and passed the blunt back to her.

"He can't keep me in."

"Shit. I would have had you hemmed up in the house."

"Trust me. He tries sometimes."

"I understand why. I didn't know that you liked to smoke."

"Yea. I do, but Lamar isn't into it like that, so I don't do it much."

"Oh, I know. Bruh only do it when we out."

"Yep, but if I could do it more often, I would."

"Shit. All I do is smoke, so if you ever want to blow one, just hit me and I'll come through and smoke you out shorty."

"Alright. Well I know my girls are waiting so I got to go."

"Aight here." Niko handed her a bag with weed in it. "This is for you and your people."

"Oh, nah you don't have to."

"Nah you good shorty. There's plenty more where that came from."

"Ok. Thanks." Aleyah said. She hopped out of the jeep and walked towards the pizza restaurant.

Chapter 24

Riley

Riley was happy to make it home to her bae after a night of partying, so Jamir could give her some of that good he always gives her. He was already there when she made it home. He told her to take a shower and meet him in the bedroom. She did as he asked and he got in the bed and laid pipe to her like it was his job. He gave it to her like he was making twenty-five thousand dollars to put the d on her. He gave it to her like that night was his last night on earth and his last wish was to give her the d. He put her in positions Riley didn't know she could get in. Jamir had her singing in high octave's as he put his pound game on her. He demanded that she say his name, he demanded that she tell him she loved him, and he demanded again that she would have his baby.

Riley froze as she reached her peak, "Jamir! Yes! I love you. I will have your baby." she cried out as she creamed.

"Oooo you're wet bae. That's the shit I like." he said to her as he continued to lay his pipe into her savagely. The sounds her peach made as he dug into her turned him on more and made him get even more aggressive.

"Oooo shit Jamir!" Riley moaned out.

"Uh huh. Take this d bae." he said to her.

"Ah stay right there."

"You love this d?"

"I love the d bae." Riley said.

"You love it when I beat this pussy?" Jamir asked.

"Yessss. I love it." she moaned. Jamir spread her legs open and went to work on her peach until he busted in her.

"Uhhh I love you!" she moaned as she felt him release into her. "I know you do." he said between breaths. He wiped sweat from his forehead. "Come on. Let's take a shower. I got to get up in the morning." he said.

"Alright. You got to help me change these sheets first." Riley said as she touched the huge wet spot in the middle.

"Yea that's all you." Jamir said. Riley laughed and then Jamir said, "This dick had you like an ocean girl."

Riley laughed again and said, "Be quiet Jamir." she pulled he wet sheets off the bed, and then she pulled a fresh set out of her closet.

"If I didn't have to work in the morning I would give you some more." he said as they put a fresh fitted sheet on the bed.

"I would let you." Riley said flirtatiously.

"Stop looking at me like that. I know you want it, but I can't bae."

"Yes, you can." she said as they put a fresh flat sheet on the bed. They put the pillows and the blanket back on the bed and then they headed to the bathroom. Jamir smacked her backside before turning on the shower water. Riley reached down and started rubbing his manhood as he adjusted the water.

"Bae, stop." he said.

Riley giggled and kept rubbing as he turned the shower on. She felt him starting to swell. He stepped away from her and told her to get in. He followed her and then she touched him again.

"See I tried to stop you, but you want to keep playing. I don't want to hear anything about me stopping once I get started either." he chuckled.

He bent her over and slid into Riley in the shower. He knew he was going to damn near kill Riley because he was even more savage the second time around. Riley held onto the wall as Jamir beat her peach up again. When it was all over, Riley wanted to put ice on her box because it was throbbing so bad.

"I told you to leave me alone." Jamir chuckled as Riley wobbled to the bed.

Riley giggled. "It's not funny. I think I need some ice."

"I bet you do. I beat that thing up real good." he laughed.

"You did."

"You like that shit."

"I do."

They laid down and Riley curled up in his arms. She couldn't have been happier with Jamir. Everything was working out the way she wanted it to.

***

Riley got dressed and headed to the gym to meet her sister shortly after Jamir left the next morning. She couldn't believe how much her peach was still throbbing the next morning. She regretted asking for the second round the night before. She knew that she could only handle Jamir once. She was questioning her decision to kick off the second round with Jamir as her and Raelyn were walking to the stair climber machines at the gym. After they began walking, Riley said, "Eazy's party was lit as usual."

"Yea it was, and not one fight popped off." Raelyn said.

"I know. What do you think was up with Aleyah and that dude?" Riley asked.

"I don't know, but she was outside with him for a while."

"I noticed that. Haven't we seen him before the party at her house?"

"I feel like we have, but I can't put my finger on it."

"Anyways. You've been distant lately sister, so that means you have secrets. What's up?" Riley asked.

"Huh?" Raelyn responded.

"Don't huh me. What's up?"

"I'm messing with Laron again."

"What? Since when?"

"Like a month ago."

"After you almost got shot over him?"

"Yes, but they are not together anymore."

"Oh, I see. You would die for the dick, huh?" Riley said with a chuckle.

"Shut up sister. I could say the same about you."

"Whatever. Me and Jamir are in a good place. We are happy."

"But are you together?"

"Yes, we are together."

"He said that?"

"Basically."

"Have you been to his place yet?"

"No. Because he is always at mine. I gave him a key."

"You did what, Riley?"

"He basically lives with me." Riley said.

"You got him staying with you sister?" Raelyn asked.

"Yes. He has stuff at my house. He is there almost every night now. I'm in love."

Raelyn exhaled and said, "Ok Riley. Well me and Laron are taking it slow. I have been to his new place, and Paris is out of the picture for real this time."

"So, you think?"

"I know for sure this time. He showed me the paperwork. They are divorced. We love each other. We always have."

"Alright. Well, you're not in a love triangle anymore."

"But you are."

"No, I'm not. He's not with her. She is just jealous that he has moved on. She needs to get over it because that stupid bitch is going to be real mad when she finds out that I am pregnant."

"Hold up. What?" Raelyn stopped the machine and climbed down.

"You're pregnant again Riley?"

"Yep. He told me that he wanted me to have his baby."

"During sex?"

"Um hum. A few times." Riley said and then she stopped her machine and climbed down. She started pat drying the sweat on her face with a white towel.

"Ah Riley. You can't be believing a dude when he is trying to get his nut. He will say anything. Especially if the cookie is good."

"He meant it."

"Has he told you that he loves you?"

"He hasn't said the words, but he shows me."

"I guess I should say congrats sister."

"Thank you."

"You know mom and dad are going to be pissed if you show up with a baby on the way, and no husband." Raelyn said as she pat dried her sweaty face.

"We are grown now. Mom and dad will just have to get over it. Me and Jamir are going to get married in our own time. I'm telling you everything is good sister. Just be happy for me. We get to buy a bunch of baby stuff and you're going to be an auntie."

"Well I am going to pray for you at church on Sunday."

"You're going to church with mom and dad?"

"No. I'm going with Shawn."

"Oh. Shawn, huh?" Riley said with a smile.

"Girl, stop. Ain't nothing there."

"He seems like a really good guy."

"He is, but not for me. We are just friends. He is not my type."

"I think you're passing up on something good."

"And I think that you need to get a clue."

Riley stuck her middle finger up and stuck out her tongue.

Chapter 25

Raelyn

I looked at a couple of cars driving along side of Shawn's car on the highway. I focused in on the license plates to see if they were from out of state. It's something that I like to do when I am driving. The car that got in front of us had a North Dakota plate on it. I studied the plate and then my ears tuned into the gospel song that was playing on the radio. I listened to the lyrics as I watched green grass and green trees go buy. Summer was almost over, and I was dreading winter season.

"Church was amazing today. It has been a while since I've been." I said to Shawn.

"Yea. Everyone needs a little church in their lives in my opinion. I am glad that you came." Shawn replied.

"Thanks for inviting me. I am glad that I came too. Your mother is really nice."

"Yea. That's my lady."

"Aww sweet. Let me find out that you're a mama's boy."

"I am, but she is not a momzilla. She is not all in my business and my dating life."

"That is good because that never turns out good."

"No, it doesn't. My mom respects my privacy. I would go through hell and back for that lady though." Shawn said as he pulled up to a Red Lobster restaurant. "Is seafood good for you?"

"Absolutely."

"Good." he replied as he pulled into a parking spot. He parked the car and then he turned to me. "Thanks for coming. I really enjoyed having you there."

"You're welcome." I said with a smile. Shawn touched my face and then my chin. "You are so beautiful to me." he said and then he pulled my chin to him and kissed me. I was surprised by his gesture, but I was also stunned by how good he could kiss. It wasn't sloppy, or long. It was just right.

When he backed away from me, I said, "Um Shawn. I think I should be honest with you."

"Alright."

"I'm involved with someone, right now."

Shawn exhaled loudly and said, "You're back with that dude, right?"

"Yes."

"I figured that."

"I like you Shawn. I'm just…."

"With who you want to be with." Shawn finished my sentence.

"Yea." I said.

"Sometimes it's not about what you want. It's about what you need."

"That is true, but I'm trying to see where it's going to go. My feelings are involved."

"I understand, and it's cool. I'm not tripping. I just want you to be happy, so I support you regardless."

"Thank you."

"We are still going to eat, right?" Shawn said with a smile.

I smiled back and said, "Yes."

"We still working out tomorrow, right?" he asked.

I laughed, "Yes."

"Alright. Let's not let this little kiss get us all messed up."

I laughed. "Alright."

"Wait don't get out yet. I want to open your door for you." Shawn said.

I laughed and took off my seatbelt. Shawn got out of the car and walked over to my side and opened the door.

"Thank you." I said as I got out of the car.

"You don't have to thank me. It's what I am supposed to do."

***

I left Shawn and headed straight to Laron's place. I couldn't wait to curl up in his arms and watch television like we did every weekend that he was in town. He was going to be leaving town the next day, so I wanted to get my time in with him.

"You look good." he said when I walked in the door.

"Thank you."

"How was church?" he asked. I told him that I was going to church, but I never told him who with. I was sure he assumed I was with my family.

"It was nice." I said as I sat down on the couch.

"That is good. Are you hungry? I can order something."

"No. I am not hungry right now. maybe later."

"Ok." he said as he sat down next to me. I climbed on top of him and kissed him. I wanted to skip all the small talk. I was in the mood to make love. I started unbuttoning his pants. He smiled and slid his hand under my dress and rubbed my backside. I stood up and took my panties off while he pulled his pants and underwear down to his ankles. I climbed back on top of him and placed his manhood inside of me.

"Mmmm." I moaned as I felt him. I kissed him as I bounced on him.

"Damn babe. This is one of the reasons why I love you so much."

I smiled and continued to make love to my man until we were both tired.

***

I woke up in the middle of the night to use the bathroom. I walked back through his dark apartment and slid in the bed. For the first time, I felt comfortable and safe. I didn't feel like I needed to check the apartment for an intruder. Laron was lying on his back when I got in the bed. He turned over, wrapped his arms around me, and pulled me to him. Without opening his eyes, he said, "If I asked you to marry me, would you?" he asked.

"You just got divorced."

"I know."

"So. Don't you think it's too soon to get married again?" I asked.

"No. It's never too soon when you really love someone, and I really love you, so would you?"

"I would."

"No bullshit?"

"Seriously."

Laron squeezed me tighter and kissed my lips. He didn't say another word. He just drifted off to sleep and so did I.

Chapter 26

Aleyah

Aleyah sat down at the sandwich shop table and looked around the brown themed restaurant. There was only a couple of people in the place. A Caucasian guy was sitting in a booth looking at his phone with a foot-long sandwich in front of him. There was a brown skin girl wearing all black sitting in a booth by the window looking at an iPad. It looked to Aleyah like the girl was on her break from working; judging by the name tag pinned to her shirt.

Eazy walked in a couple of minutes after her. She saw him walking through the door. The powder blue shirt he was wearing made his mahogany brown skin more noticeable. She felt a slight queasiness in the pit of her stomach. He seemed to have that affect every time she saw him. He was even more attractive than he was when they were younger. She stood up and to hug him. After they embraced, he said, "Let's get some food."

Aleyah followed him to the counter and they both ordered sandwiches. Eazy paid the bill, and then they sat down to eat and talk.

"How have you been?" Eazy asked Aleyah.

"I've been really good Eazy. How about you?" she responded.

"I've been maintaining."

"That's good. You look handsome and usual."

"Thanks. You look gorgeous as always."

"Thanks."

"I'm glad that you're back."

"I'm happy to be back."

"How was the ATL?"

"It was nice. People are nice down there. I love to see how our people are thriving down there."

"Yea. I have never been down there."

"You got to go. You will love it."

"I plan to."

"Let me know when you do. I can tell you some places to check out."

"Cool. How's married life treating you?"

"It's been good." Aleyah said cheerfully.

Eazy nodded his head. "Are you sure?"

"Of course."

"Doesn't seem like it to me. Sounds like your faking it."

"I'm happy Eazy." Aleyah laughed.

"Ok. If you say so." he smiled.

"Whatever." she smiled back.

"Nah. I'm just saying. You can't lie to me." he chuckled. Eazy was low key flirting and Aleyah was doing the same. Neither of them had stopped smiling since he walked in.

"I'm not lying." Aleyah said. "Anyways how are you and the baby mom?"

"You know how she is. Same. Driving me insane." he said.

Aleyah laughed and said, "You two were meant for each other."

"Now you know that's bullshit." he said.

Aleyah laughed again. "You know that you were supposed to have my baby." he said.

Aleyah swallowed down the food she was chewing and said, "Don't start."

"What? You know how we felt about each other growing up."

"Yea and that was a long time ago."

"Those feelings haven't changed Aleyah."

"I'm married."

"You only got married to cover up your pregnancy. You and I both know that."

"I love my husband."

"You love me, and you always have. We don't have to hide it anymore. We are grown now. I know Lamar is not making you happy."

"Yes, he is. He is a good guy."

"Doesn't mean he is right for you. You and him ain't got the chemistry and bond that me and you got. He doesn't make you smile the way I do, and I am sure he ain't fucking you right."

Aleyah rolled her eyes. "Don't roll your eyes. You know that it's true." he said.

"It's not."

"You haven't been the same since you've been with him. You used to be fun. He dims your inner light."

"What are you trying to say? That I am boring? I'm still a lot of fun. Just not the fun that you're used to. We are fine. He does make me smile, and we have an amazing relationship."

"Um hum. Who do you think that you are talking to? I know you. I knew you when you were just a nappy headed little girl with pig tails who talked too damn much. All that shit is a front. You're just existing in that relationship, and doing whatever to try to make it work because you don't want to disappoint your parents."

"Eazy. Stop. I am fine. My marriage is fine." Aleyah laughed and then she looked down at her phone. "I have to go." she said.

"Alright. Oh yea. I'm having a barbeque get together at my place in a few weeks. It's an end of summer jam just for friends and some family. There are going to be drinks, food, good music, positive people. The twins are coming. You and your hubby should come through."

"I don't know."

Eazy chuckled. "Why? Your man still doesn't like me? It's cool. Tell him that I'm not going to take his woman and he has nothing to worry about." Easy said jokingly.

Aleyah smacked her lips and said, "Stop."

"Alright. You should still come through. It's going to be lit."

"I'll think about it."

"Alright cool."

They stood up and Eazy gave Aleyah a tight bear hug. "I missed you girl." he said.

"I missed you too." she said. Eazy followed Aleyah out of the restaurant and walked her to her car. When Aleyah pulled off, she answered a call coming from Niko.

"Hey beautiful. You busy? Come smoke with me."

"Hey Niko. I'm not busy. Where should I meet you?"

"Let's meet at the lake, and you can hop in with me."

"Alright it should take me about fifteen minutes to get there."

Chapter 27
Aleyah

Aleyah made it there in ten minutes and parked. Niko pulled his Jeep up behind her car. Aleyah got out of her car, locked the doors, and got into Niko's truck. He cracked the windows and pulled off.

"There is a low-key spot around the corner I like to smoke at."

"Ok." she said.

"Sup with you beautiful?" he asked.

"Nothing I was off work today, so I decided to hang out a for a few hours before I go to pick little man up from daycare. This is exactly what I needed to unwind."

"I understand. I am off work today too. I was just bending some corners and decided to hit you up. I figured you would want to blow one with me. Is Lamar at work?"

"Yea. Where is Faye?

"She is at work too."

Niko drove up the block, turned the corner, and parked by some trees. He pulled the blunt out of the ashtray and handed it to Aleyah.

"Ladies first." he said. Aleyah giggled and took the blunt. She took a pull and went into a coughing fit. "Yea that's that gas." Niko said while laughing. "Are you ok?"

Aleyah started laughing when she got herself together. "Damn Niko. Where did you get this?" she asked while wiping tears from her eyes.

"My boy got it from Cali." he said. Aleyah handed the blunt back to him.

"What? you scared to hit it again?" Niko chuckled.

"I'm not messing with that." Aleyah said, and then she laughed.

Niko took the blunt from her and said, "Aight. come here. let me give you a shot gun." He took a long pull from the blunt. He pulled her face to him and blew smoke towards her lips. Aleyah puckered her lips to inhale a little of the smoke. She inhaled the smoke and before she could blow the smoke back out, he kissed her. She accepted the kiss without resisting. Aleyah released the smoke from her mouth while kissing Niko. They share tongues and sucked on each other's lips for several seconds and then they pulled away from each other.

"Do you know how long I've been waiting to do that?" Niko asked.

"Wow Niko." Aleyah said.

"I know, but you're sexy as fuck to me. You always have been. I wanted you before we had the little situation at your place. I mean I was never going to say anything, but that situation gave me an in. Trust me, if I wasn't attracted to you, I wouldn't have done it. I just wanted to experience you."

"That is just something me and my husband do together."

"It's something that you like. You bored with him. Bruh wasn't into that kind of stuff. Trust me I know. He does it for you, and you do it for the excitement, and that is what I like about you."

"Yea well outside of what we do together, nothing is happening."

Niko sat up and leaned closer to Aleyah. "Are you sure? Are you sure you don't want me? Because I think you want me." he said.

Aleyah felt her plum throb a little as she felt his hand touch her face to kiss her again. As she kissed him, his hand slid down her neck to her breast. He rubbed her nipple a little and then she stopped him. "Um. I've got to go."

"I'm saying we've already had each other, so it couldn't hurt. I can please you and you know it. Just think about it."

***

Aleyah drove home before going to pick up little man. She had a couple of hours before she had to get him, and she knew Lamar was going to be home early. He was standing in the kitchen already showered and changed out of his work clothes when she walked into the house. Aleyah walked up to him and kissed him.

"Hey babe." he said.

"Hey." she said back.

Aleyah touched the crotch of his basketball shorts and the she bent down in front of him. "Damn what's up?" he asked as she took his manhood out of his boxers and put it into her mouth. She didn't respond to him and he didn't stop her. He let her do her thing. Aleyah sucked him until he was stiff and then she stood up and said, "I want you to fuck me."

"Damn. Ok." Lamar said. Aleyah hopped up onto the counter and pulled his hips to her. He put his manhood into her and being pumping in and out of her. She moaned and leaned her head back.

"Go faster." she whispered. Lamar sped up the pace which made her moan louder.

"Yes, right there, fuck me harder." Aleyah moaned. Lamar pounder harder.

"Mmm, yes, grab my neck." she said.

"Huh?" he asked.

"Grab my neck and tell me it's yours."

"Babe what are you on?"

"Do it." she demanded.

He did what she asked. He put his hand on her neck and told her that it was his. "Ah yea. Like that." she moaned. "Don't stop. I want you to make me cum." she said.

"Babe. I'm about to cum." he said.

"No. Hold it. Hold it for me." she moaned.

"I can't babe."

"No." she said.

"Shit." he grunted and let himself go. Aleyah opened her eyes and looked up at the ceiling. She looked at him as he stepped back. She slid off the counter.

"What was that about?"

"Nothing." she said as she walked past him towards the bathroom. "I'm about to go and get little man."

Chapter 28

Aleyah

Aleyah walked through the office carrying a container of food that she got for lunch. She sat down at her desk and set her food in front of her. She was eager to dig into the barbeque platter. The smell was making her hungrier. She felt her phone buzz in her pocket. She pulled her phone out of her pocket and looked down at the text message from Eazy and smiled.

E: Good morning. I was thinking about you.

A: I was thinking about you too.

E: Do you have to pick up little man after work today?

A: No.

E: You should meet me in the old neighborhood at the park.

A: Ok.

Aleyah smiled again and put her phone into her pocket. She opened her box of yummy goodness and began to eat. She thought about Eazy the rest of her day at work. She remembered thinking about him a lot while she was living in Atlanta, but she had taught herself to forget about him after a while. Being back home and back around him and the twins had made it all fresh again.

Right after work, she drove to the park on the Southside in their old neighborhood to meet Eazy. She got out of her car after she parked it, then met Eazy on the sidewalk.

"Hi Eazy." she said with a smile.

"Hi Aleyah." he responded before hugging her.

They walked and talked about work for a little while until they made it to the playground.

"Remember when we used to come to this park?"

"Yes, and the twins would always argue about who was going to get the swing first because one of the swings was always broke."

"Yup. My sisters were a trip sometimes."

"They still are."

"I know." Eazy said. Aleyah started walking to the swing set and Eazy followed her. They both sat in the swings.

"I can't believe they got that one fixed. Gosh this park brings back so many memories."

"I know. Remember we shared our first kiss behind that building?"

"I remember. The twins caught us and we were scared they were going to tell on us, so we bribed them with some candy." They laughed.

"I was scared your dad was going to kill me. I couldn't have Deacon Carter on my tail."

Aleyah laughed.

"I remember in high school when we all snuck out to go to that party and got caught."

"Yes. Man, I never heard the end of it."

"All of us were grounded forever." Aleyah said.

"I know, and all I was mad about was the fact that I couldn't see or talk to you." Eazy said.

"We were best friends."

"I never stopped loving you."

"I know."

"We should have been together and married with a baby."

"It's too late now."

"No, it's not."

"Eazy. Your baby's mother is my best friend, so there is no way that can happen, but we will always be best friends."

"Fuck her. We ain't together, and we are never going to be together. I never told you, but she cheated on me."

"What?"

"Yup. On top of all the nagging and drama she put me through. That was the main reason we broke up."

"She never told me that."

"I'm sure that she didn't. I haven't been in a relationship with a woman since."

"That's crazy Eazy."

"I knew that I had made a mistake being with her. We were young, and I was dumb and full of cum. I should have gone against the grain and stuck with you."

"Things have changed. I'm not the same person I was in high school."

"Neither am I. Look, I am not trying to get you to cheat on your husband or be disloyal to your friend. I am trying to get you to consider happiness with someone that you love. I'm alright with being friends. I never want to do anything to jeopardize our friendship. If you stay with dude, I am cool with that and I support you. I guess I just felt like when you left I never had the chance to tell you how I felt about you, so I didn't want to miss the opportunity. I love you."

"I love you too Eazy, and I always will."

"You better." he said. Eazy helped Aleyah stand up. He wrapped his arms around her and gave her a bear hug. He gave her a quick kiss on the lips.

"I got to get home and get dinner ready." Aleyah said.

"You cook now?" Eazy asked.

"Um hum and I am good at it too."

"Wow check you out. You'll have to cook something for me sometime."

"I got you."

"Aight don't forget my party in a few weeks."

"I won't."

Chapter 29

Raelyn

I stood back and watched Shawn struggle with his last squat. I smiled and gave him some encouragement.

"You got it."

"Arrgghh." he grunted as he pushed the weight back up from a squatting position to a standing position. The weight made a loud sound when he set in back on the bar. Shawn bent over to catch his breath.

I giggled. "Are you alright?" I asked.

"You're going to kill me girl." he said through breaths.

"No, I'm not. You said that you didn't want me to go easy on you."

"I know, but I didn't know that it was going to be this hard."

"You'll be alright. Getting back in shape is always hard, but it will get better."

"What's next?" he asked.

"We need to stretch."

"You know what? You should be a personal trainer." Shawn said as we sat down on the mat to start stretching.

"You think so?" I asked. We sat facing each other with our legs spread open. I grabbed his arms and pulled his towards me. He winced when he felt his inner thigh muscles stretch. He lifted and pulled me towards him.

He said, "Yea. You're good at it."

"I don't know. It's a thought. I do love working out and eating healthy." I said as I stretched.

"It will give you something else to do besides bartending." he said as I pulled him towards me again.

"True." I responded.

"Where are we going after this?" he asked.

"To get a nice delicious protein shake." I said.

"We can't get some steak and potatoes." he asked.

"No, and if I find out your eating potatoes. I am going to kill you." I flicked him in the arm.

"That hurt." he said and pulled me to him aggressively. I fell onto my back and started laughing. He stood up and then he extended his hand to help me stand up. I stood up and said, "Promise me. No potatoes. Only vegetables and fruits."

"I don't want to, but I promise. Thanks for working out with me and helping me to get back to the way I used to be before my ex started stressing me out. I put on most of my weight stress eating." he said.

"Stress eating is the worst because you just eat anything, and comfort foods are addicting." I responded. We started walking towards the gym entrance, so we could leave.

"Yup. I was all about the comfort foods. My favorite was a bag of chips, a large pizza, and a two-liter bottle of soda."

"Ew. That is heart attack central."

"I know. That's why I am happy to have you around. To help me get back on track."

"Well, I am happy to be around to keep you alive. Geesh."

Shawn laughed. "When is our next session?"

"Friday morning. Does that work for you?"

"Nothing better than working out before handling ignorant fools at the club."

I laughed as he opened my car door for me. I got into my car and heard my phone ringing. I picked it up and saw an unsaved number, so I answered it.

"Hello?"

"Raelyn." I remembered that voice.

"Paris?" I said.

"Yes. Um.." she said. I frowned, and before she could finish her sentence, I hung up.

Shawn got into my car and saw the look on my face.

"What's wrong?" he asked.

"That was my dude's ex."

"Why would she be calling you?"

"I don't know, but I hung up on her. I will be asking him about it."

***

Later that day, I was sitting at home waiting for Laron to pick me up. We had plans to go to the movies that evening after he finished up a photo shoot for a local singer. My phone buzzed. It was a text message from Laron telling me that he was in front of my building. I walked out of my apartment and locked my door. I got into the car without a smile or a hug.

"What's wrong?" he asked.

"Are you messing with Paris again?"

"Huh? No. Why the hell would you ask me that?"

"Because she called my phone today, and I am trying to figure out why!" I yelled. "Is she lurking for her husband again!?"

"No babe. I swear. I don't know why she would call you. I am not messing with her. I don't even talk to her anymore. Both of us changed our numbers and blocked each other from social media after our divorce."

"Laron, you have lied to me before. Am I supposed to believe you?"

"I swear babe. You can believe me. I don't deal with her at all. Period."

"So, if I call her back, she will say the same thing?" I asked.

"I swear to God she will. We are no more. I don't know why she called you. I don't even know why she still has your number." he said. I folded my arms across my chest.

He said, "Swear babe. Please hear me. I wouldn't do that to you." I took a deep breath and exhaled. "Ok. I'm sorry." I felt my heart rate beginning to slow down.

"Can we go now?" he asked.

"Yes."

Chapter 30

Riley

Bitch I told you to stay away from my husband!

Riley read social media instant message again. The green dot next to the girl's name let her know that the girl was online. Riley had blocked Jamir's ex-wife Kiesha from her page, but Kiesha was messaging Riley from another page. Riley smirked and responded to the message.

Beat it bitch. Why are you contacting me from another page, when I blocked you? Get a life bitch. He ain't yours!

He is mine bitch! We are still married!

Raelyn frowned and responded.

You're crazy! He don't want you! He loves me and that is why he is always at my house all the time!

Bitch he lives with me! He is only at your house when I kick his ass out! You ain't nothing but a side hoe! He's using you bitch! You're dumb as fuck!

We are together, so get over it! Leave us alone!

We are still very married! If we aren't, then why did we just celebrate our wedding anniversary in Mexico? Did you think he went out of town for his health? Why am I pregnant with our second child right now? He only uses you when he is mad at me! He doesn't want you honey! We are still very happily married you dumb bitch! Since you think that I am lying, here are the receipts!

Raelyn's stomach dropped as pictures started coming through the email app. Recent pictures of Kiesha and Jamir looking happy together on the beach, at restaurants, and in a hotel room. She could tell by Jamir's haircut that they were recent. He had just gotten his haircut with a design in the front before he had left out of town. She also sent an ultra sound picture, and then Kiesha sent another message.

Here are pictured of us in Mexico. Here is the ultra sound picture of our baby. You're a dumb ass hoe. He is home now, and we are fine! Oh, and I got your videos, you nasty bitch! If you don't leave him alone, I will post them all over social media.

Kiesha sent one of the videos of Riley giving Jamir head on video.

He's mine bitch, so you beat it!

"Uuuuggh!" Riley screamed. She called Jamir, but no answer. She called a few more times, but it went to voicemail. She called again, and then he answered.

"Jamir what is this shit about you Kiesha still being together!" Riley yelled into the phone.

"Riley let me explain." Jamir said.

"Tell her!" she heard Kiesha yell in the background."

"I am Kiesha! Calm down!" he yelled.

"Look me and my wife.."

"We're together!" she yelled into the phone.

"What do you mean you and your wife!? You told me that y'all weren't together!" Riley yelled into the phone.

"We are, um, working things out."

"Working things out!?"

"Yea bitch!" Kiesha yelled. "Now get off his phone!"

"You told me that you weren't with her! You told me that she was crazy and that you wanted to be with me Jamir!"

"I never said that." Jamir said.

"Ha! He never wanted to be with you!" Kiesha yelled.

Tell that bitch fuck her! Does she know that I am pregnant with your child!?"

"Pregnant?" he asked.

"Yes! I'm pregnant! Did you tell that bitch that!?"

"Are you sure? Is it even mine?"

"Is it yours? Are you serious?!" Riley yelled.

"I never fucked you without a condom."

"Oh my God! You're going to sit up there and lie Jamir! You know damn well this is your baby!"

"I don't know. I don't know who you were fucking with." Jamir said.

"You know damn well I was only messing with you Jamir!?" Riley yelled.

"Ha! You're tryna keep him with a baby! This hoe is stupid is hell! She ain't pregnant!" Kiesha yelled.

"Kiesha be quiet!" he yelled.

"Really Jamir!?" Riley yelled.

"I don't know. You could have been messing with someone else. I already have a baby on the way. I'm not having any more kids."

"I can't believe you Jamir! You're really not going to claim your baby!?"

"Yea you heard him! Our baby is on the way! Go and find the real daddy hoe!" Kiesha yelled.

"Look. I just need to come and get my stuff your place." he said.

"Really? That's it!?" Riley asked.

"Yea that's it! Bitch bye!" Kiesha yelled and then the phone hung up. Riley slammed her phone down on her coffee table and began to cry.

Chapter 31

Aleyah

Aleyah opened the door to her house to greet her best friend Karina.

"Leeeeyah!" Karina screeched.

"Triiinaaa!" Aleyah yelled. They hugged each other tightly. Aleyah stepped back so she could get a look at her friend. She is taller than Aleyah, has a light brown complexion, and is much thicker than Aleyah. She has a small waist and wide hips, and has an extremely voluptuous butt. She looks like one of those model chicks from reality television.

"You look good bestie!" Aleyah said as Karina turned in a circle.

"Thank you! You too friend. I missed you." she said.

They hugged again and then Aleyah closed the door. As they walked to the couch to sit down Aleyah said, "It's about time that you made time for me. I was about to replace you as my best friend."

"Shut up! You will never replace me." Karina said.

"I know you don't drink much so would you like some water?" Aleyah asked.

"I would love some."

"I see your keeping that waist tight."

"Yes girl. I've been waist training. I've got my social media modeling life going, so I got to stay fit. It's all about the small waist and big asses these days."

"Yes, it is and I don't have either."

"Sorry, but you have no ass at all." Karina said. Aleyah laughed and said, "Be quiet, so why haven't I seen you since I've been back?"

"I apologize. I've been so busy with work, school, fitness, and my princess. I haven't been able to find the time for myself lately."

Aleyah said, "I understand."

"You look good though. What have you been up to since you've been back?"

"Mostly working, but I've been hanging out with the twins and their friends since my best friend has been too busy. We are going out tonight just for a girls night. Do you want to come?

"I wish that I could. I have too much homework piled up."

"I understand."

"How's the hubby and little man?"

"They're good. You know us. Mostly at home and work. I wish we would get out more."

"You two have always been busy, but when you do go out, you always do it big."

"Not as much as we used to."

"Uh oh. Someone doesn't sound happy."

"I don't know what's wrong girl. I haven't been feeling him lately. It feels like, I don't know, like it's missing something. Like that passion when you're really into someone. It's just not there in between us."

"Wait. Aren't y'all swingers? I thought life was always exciting for y'all?"

"We are, and it was. It spiced things up for a while, but it seems to be the only time we are having fun. Other than that, we are at work, or at home sitting on the couch watching television. It's been like that for a couple of years now."

"Y'all just need to switch it up again and put some fire back into the marriage."

"Well, we swung an episode with Niko and his girl."

"Fine ass Niko?"

"Yup."

"When?"

"A couple of months ago."

"Damn. What was that like?"

"It was good. We had a lot of fun. We kicked it like old times. Went to a freaky party a few nights before, and then they came through and played cards with us. We got drunk and high and then we did our thing. Niko felt good. I'm sure Lamar enjoyed Faye."

"Damn. I haven't done anything like that since that one time with y'all a long time ago."

"We haven't done anything fun since Niko unless you come back." Aleyah said and laughed.

"Uh -uh. I'm not trying to be wrapped up with y'all. That was a one-time deal."

"I know. I was just playing." Aleyah said.

"Plus, I am trying to clear my karma, so I can hook a good man." Karina said.

"Um. You had a good man. You need to change your attitude, so you can keep a good man."

Karina smacked her lips. "My attitude ain't that bad."

"Let you tell it. You're high maintenance, spoiled, and a drama queen."

"Now you sound like my baby daddy. Maybe Niko would like it."

"Um. No."

"What you mean no? Sounds like you're trying to save him for yourself."

"No. I'm not. I'm just saying. I don't think you're his type. You're a drama queen. He likes a laid-back type of woman that can go with the flow. You would be complaining too much."

"Yea whatever. I'm not a drama queen. I think you want to fuck him solo."

"No, I don't."

"Um hum. Yes, you do, and part of me doesn't blame you. I mean, I know your husband's issues and he wasn't that bad when we did our thing, but I'm sure he can't beat that pussy like Niko, and that's what you want."

Aleyah laughed. "Ew, listen to you. Nasty. Shut up." she said.

"I'm serious. I know girl. I like getting my thing tapped like that. I miss getting it like that from Eazy." Karina laughed. "Anyways. I want you to meet my homegirl. I met her in school while you were gone. She is so dope. You are going to love her."

"Oh, so you've been trying to replace me?" Aleyah asked.

"No one will take my besties place, but she has been around. She was there for me when me and Eazy broke up. She's always helpful with Princess. We should all go out together soon for girl's night when I don't have homework piled up a mountain high."

"Ok. Sounds like a plan."

"Aright, well I've got to go girl. I've got to go and get Princess and go home." They stood up and hugged.

"I love you girl." Karina said.

"I love you more." Aleyah said.

***

Aleyah text messaged Niko while sitting at the dinner table with Raelyn and Cherry.

Are you out tonight?

Yup! Are you?

Yes. Where are you at?

I'm at where ever you're at beautiful. You tryna hit this gas with me?

Yea. We'll be going to the club down the street in a few minutes.

Aight text me you're location.

Aleyah text messaged the location of the nightclub and then turned her attention back to the ladies. They were asking the waitress for the bill.

"I hate that Riley and Taji aren't here."

"Yea. Riley said that she wasn't in the mood, and Taji is out of town." Raelyn said.

"What's wrong with Riley?"

"I don't know. She didn't want to talk about it."

"If you ask me, that dude has something to do with it." Cherry said.

"I am sure that he does." Raelyn said. She took the bill from the waitress and handed her some money. "I got dinner for the both of y'all tonight." she said and then she told the waitress to keep the change.

"Thank you." Cherry said.

"No problem. Happy birthday girl."

"Thanks Raelyn." Aleyah said.

"It's nothing girl. Y'all ready to go and dance this meal off?"

"Yes." Cherry said.

The three ladies stood up and walked outside to get their cars out of Valet parking. They followed each other a few blocks down to the nightclub. After getting parked they headed inside and went straight to the bar for drinks. Aleyah bought double shots of patron for the three of them, and then followed it up with glasses of wine for the three ladies. They went to the dance floor to dance and then Aleyah went back to the bar for another double shot.

"She better slow down." Cherry said.

"I know. She has been on one lately." Raelyn said.

Aleyah walked back swaying and dancing to the music with another glass of wine in hand.

"Girl, you are already on your second glass of wine? We have only been here for like twenty minutes." Cherry said.

"I know. I am just having fun."

"Yea, well don't get sloppy." Raelyn said.

"I know. I got this." Aleyah said as she kept dancing. Raelyn pulled out her phone and took a few video clips of them for her social media page, and then she took a few selfie photos with them. After she was done, Aleyah pulled out her phone to read a text message from Niko.

Hey boo. I'm in the building.

Aleyah looked up from her phone and searched the club for Niko. She spotted him at the bar. She told the girls that she would be right back and then she walked over to the bar.

"You look good." Niko said and then he gave her a long, warm hug.

"You look good too." Aleyah said to Niko. She could feel his arm around her waist. He hadn't moved it yet.

"What you, drinking?" Aleyah asked.

"Oh. You're buying?" Niko smiled.

"Yup." she smiled.

"Aight. What have you been drinking?"

"Patron shots."

"Aight. I'm cool with that." Niko said.

Aleyah ordered Patron shots from the bartender. They took the shots and then Niko asked, "What you on tonight?"

"Going home after this."

"Or, you can come with me."

"Boy stop." Aleyah laughed and pushed his shoulder.

"Aight, well let's go smoke."

"Ok."

Aleyah wobbled back to the dance floor to tell the girls that she was leaving for the night.

"What's up with you and dude? Y'all were all over each other." Raelyn said.

"Oh, it's nothing. He is my husband's friend. He's cool." Aleyah said.

"I know that, but it just seems a little flirtatious to me." Raelyn said.

"Girl no. He is just a friend of ours. You wouldn't understand." Aleyah said.

"I don't think your husband would understand his friend being all over you like that." Raelyn said.

"Girl. He doesn't care. Anyways I am about to go." Aleyah said.

"Alright." Raelyn said.

Aleyah walked out the club with Niko and followed him to his Jeep. After they smoked for a few minutes, he said, "You should come with me."

"Come with you where?"

"To go chill." he said.

"We *are* chilling."

"Aleyah, why are you acting like you don't want it as much as I want it? We've already been together."

"I know."

"Ok then, let's do this one time, and then we can forget it forever."

He put his hand on her leg and leaned in to kiss her. She kissed him back and let him feel her up until he touched her peach. She let him rub her peach while they shared a kiss. The five patron shots, wine, and the marijuana had her floating. She was beyond her limit again, but aware of what she was doing. Niko stopped and asked, "Are you down?"

"Yea." Aleyah replied.

"Aight cool."

Niko sat back in his seat, turned the key in the ignition, put the car in reverse to back out of the parking spot, and then put the car in drive to pull out of the parking lot.

Chapter 32

Aleyah

Niko grabbed a fist full of Aleyah's hair and smack her butt. The sound of the smack echoed through the hotel room.

"Ah!" Aleyah moaned out loud.

"You like that?" Niko asked.

"Yes Niko." Aleyah moaned. She was in a zone and she was loving Niko's pound game. She knew that he would go even harder with her husband not around.

"Damn this pussy good girl." Niko said as he continued to thrust aggressively into Aleyah. He had her bent over doggy style in the King size hotel bed. Aleyah looked back at him, smiled, and said, "Fuck this pussy good."

"Yea?" Niko asked as he pounded even harder.

"Yes, like that." Aleyah said through heavy breathing and moans. She grabbed the sheets and bounced back on Niko. He responded to her by smacking her butt again.

"Ahhh." she moaned again. Niko pulled out and told her to flip over.

"I wanna taste that pussy again." he said. Aleyah rolled over onto her back and spread her legs open wide. She started rubbing her peach in a circular motion.

"Mmmm." Niko groaned as he watched her rubbing herself. He was rubbing his manhood while watching her. "Spread it open." he said. She spread her lower lips open with two fingers.

He bent down in front of her and said, "Look at this pretty pussy." Niko put his tongue on her pearl and flicked it a few times before sucking on it.

"Shit Niko." Aleyah moaned as she lost herself to an orgasm.

Niko watched her shake and shiver with a smile on his face and then he dipped his finger into her and said,

"Taste your pussy." He put his finger in her mouth. She sucked her juices off his finger and smiled. He smiled back, stood up, and put his manhood back into her. Niko put one of her legs on his shoulder and begin plunging into her wet center relentlessly. Aleyah grabbed Niko's butt and helped him plunge deeper.

"Yes deeper." Aleyah moaned.

"Um hum." Niko moaned. "Sexy mutha fucka. I'm going to make you cum again." "Yea?"

"Yea. You want that don't you?"

"Yes. Please make me cum again." He put his thumb on her pearl and began rubbing it as he pounded into her. He started short stroking her spot as he rubbed her clit.

"Shit Niko." she moaned again.

"Shit what? You're about to cum again?"

"Yeeeessss. I'm cuming." Aleyah moaned out. Niko was giving her everything she wanted sexually and more. She knew that he was going to be good, but she wasn't expecting it to be *that* good. Aleyah's orgasm rocked her body. She shivered and then her legs started feeling weak.

"I got those legs shaking. You can take some more." he groaned. He pushed her legs towards the headboard and went even harder into her. She grabbed the sheets and cried out, "Ahhhh!"

"Yea. There you go. Take this dick sexy." Niko moaned. Aleyah leaned her head back and told him to go deeper. She was so into it that the fact that she was cheating on her husband never crossed her mind. Aleyah was focused on the sexual pleasure Niko was giving her. She begged him to go harder and deeper until he reached a peak of his own.

"Damn Aleyah." He moaned as he got his. He collapsed on top of her; sweating and breathing hard. They lay there for a few minutes and then Aleyah looked at the clock. It was a little after one o'clock in the morning. Club closing time was two o'clock, so she knew that she had to get home soon.

"I've got to go."

"I know. I'm going to take you back to your car. You should probably get cleaned up first. Are you alright to drive?"

"Yes. I am fine." Aleyah said. She stood up and walked to the bathroom to take a shower.

Chapter 33

Raelyn

I looked around the patio area of the restaurant me and Laron were having lunch at on a Saturday afternoon. There were a few other people out there with us, but it wasn't packed. The waiter walked up and asked to refill our glasses with water. He refilled them and told us that our food would be out soon. Laron looked at me and said, "The weather is beautiful."

"It is. I am sad that summer is almost over."

"It's ok. Cuddling season is coming."

I smiled. "It sure is." I looked at the ring on my finger. The diamond was sparking under the sunlight. Laron had proposed to me the night before over a candlelight dinner at his place. I said yes to the proposal.

We made love all morning and decided to go out to have lunch to celebrate our engagement. I couldn't believe that I was going to get married, and Laron was finally going to meet my family. The waiter walked back outside with plates in hand. He placed out plates of food in front of us and asked if we needed anything else. We answered no and then he walked away.

"Let's pray." Laron said. I put my hands into his and we closed our eyes and bowed our heads. After he said a prayer, we leaned over the table to share a kiss. Next thing I heard was, "Oh hell nah! Laron!" coming from the side of us, and then I saw a thick Caucasian girl with tattoos coming towards us fast.

"What the hell are you doing out here with her!? she yelled. She stormed up to him and slapped him. Laron stood up and yelled "A-yo chill!"

"Hell nah! I didn't sit around and wait for you for four years to have you cheating on me with someone else!"

"Jennifer, you are out here making a scene!"

"You damn right I am making a scene! I was walking past with my mother and I have to run into my man having lunch and kissing someone else! I waited four years for you to divorce that other chick! I am not about to sit back and let you play me!" Jennifer yelled. She swung at him again and landed a hard smack on his head. Her mother yelled, "Jennifer let's go!" Her mother grabbed her arm.

"No mom! He has me messed up! Fucking cheater! Liar!" She swung again, but Laron blocked her.

Restaurant staff rushed outside to try to diffuse the situation. Part of me couldn't believe what I was seeing, but part of me could. I slowly stood up and walked away as the argument between Laron and Jennifer was still happening. I heard her ask him who the hell I was. I heard him stuttering and stumbling over his words. I started walking towards a hotel that was a couple of blocks down, so I could get into a cab and go home. I was shaking my head the whole way. Laron came running up before I made it to the hotel.

"Raelyn!" he yelled. I heard him and kept walking. When he made it to me, he stopped in front of me. I side stepped him and kept walking. He started walking along side of me.

"Raelyn. Listen" he said between breaths.

I stopped walking and said, "What Laron?"

"Look. Just please listen. I can explain."

"Honestly I don't want to hear it. I don't want to know, and I don't care."

"Raelyn. Please." Laron said.

I took my ring off and handed it to him. "Just leave me alone." I said.

"Raelyn." he said.

"No. For real this time." I said.

"Listen I know what it looks like, but it's not that."

"Laron! This is the second time that we've been ambushed by a woman of yours! At this point, I don't care! Just leave me the fuck alone!" I yelled. I side stepped him, kept walking to the hotel, and got into a cab.

To be Continued.......

Acknowledgements

Thanks to the Creator for giving me this gift and allowing me to share it with everyone reading this book. I didn't grow up thinking that I would be an author, but the day I decided that this is what I wanted to do, I knew that God had pointed me in this direction, and I am forever grateful. I am finally doing something that I love, and I enjoy every minute of it, so I hope that you loved reading this piece of work as much as I loved writing it. Thanks to my family, friends, readers, and supporters for inspiring and encouraging me. I appreciate all of you and hope that you continue take this journey with me. As always, remember to live, laugh, and love. Smooches!

-Nia Rich

Contact

niarichbooks@gmail.com

Connect

Instagram: @Iam_niarich

Facebook: @Iam_niarich

Twitter: @Iam_niarich

Nia Rich